SEXING THE CHERRY

Jeanette Winterson was born in 1959, grew up in Lancashire and now lives in London. *Oranges Are Not the Only Fruit* won the 1985 Whitbread Award for First Novel; her adaptation of *Oranges* for BBC television has won her awards around the world, including a BAFTA for best drama. Jeanette Winterson's most recent novel is *Art & Lies*. She is also the author of *Written on the Body*, a love story; *Sexing the Cherry*, winner of the E. M. Forster Award for the American Academy for Arts and Letters; and *The Passion*, winner of the 1987 John Llewellyn Rhys Prize.

GW00502251

BY JEANETTE WINTERSON

Novels

Filmscripts

'Toads which sing madrigals, dancing princesses who fly from their tower at night, a house that is all ceilings and no floors – Jeanette Winterson's *Sexing the Cherry* is packed with strange and wonderful things. The boy Jordan and his massive adoptive mother The Dog Woman, live on the slimy banks of the River Thames in seventeenth century London.

They catch a glimpse of the first banana, experience the Civil War and witness the execution of King Charles, but these facts run alongside an extravagant fantasy . . . Jeanette Winterson's voice is startlingly poetic and original, and her imaginative feats are utterly dazzling.'

Cosmopolitan

'*Sexing the Cherry* fuses male and female voices in an exuberant blend of the historical and the fabulous. The Dog Woman, unequivocally relishing a boisterous heroism . . . occupies a hut on the banks of the Thames in seventeenth century London. She earns an eccentric living by organising fights and races for the boar-hounds she breeds. But to suggest that the novel is set in any one period or place would give a false impression, for Winterson wants to question customary thinking about what time is . . . she tells a dazzling tale, and *Sexing the Cherry* is a network of sharp and vivid stories. Their seventeenth century colouring is hardly more than incidental, for Winterson's fingers are firmly on the pulse of the 1990s . . . Her work has a solidity and point that is lodged in something firmer than fashion. *Sexing the Cherry* has a rare and winning quality: it cheers you up.'

London Review of Books

'The Dog Woman is one of the most appealing, alarming giants in literature since Gargantua, and her functions are truly Rabelaisian: as a mirror to show up other people's hypocrisy, and – brutally and satisfyingly – as a fleshy hammer to smash them to smithereens. Jeanette Winterson is as eager to rage at the human condition as any skinhead in a shopping mall, but, instead of roaring and nutting at random, she expresses her fury in one of the rarest and most unsettling of all literary genres – Gothic farce . . . The Dog Woman's foster son, Jordan, named after the river, narrates half the book, his sections alternating with his mother's. He is a voyager, the apprentice and (later) companion of the naturalist John Tradescant . . . Jordan's real-life journeys, as he narrates them, are bizarre enough. But he also travels inside his own mind . . . *Sexing the Cherry* is a rich mixture: short, but packed. There is a third ingredient, kept to the end. It is a surprise which clinches the novel, and homicidal giants will not drag it out of me.'

Sunday Times

Jeanette Winterson

SEXING THE CHERRY

VINTAGE

VINTAGE

20 Vauxhall Bridge Road, London SW1V 2SA

London Melbourne Sydney Auckland Johannesburg
and agencies throughout the world

First published by Bloomsbury Publishing Ltd 1989
Vintage edition 1990

15 16

Set in 10½/12 Sabon by Falcon Typographic Art Ltd

Printed and bound in Great Britain by
Cox & Wyman Ltd, Reading, Berks.

ISBN 0 09 974720 0

FOR MELANIE ADAMS

My thanks are due to Don and Ruth Rendell, whose hospitality gave me the space to work. To all at Bloomsbury, especially Liz Calder and Caroline Michel. And to Pat Kavanagh for her continual support.

The Hopi, an Indian tribe, have a language as sophisticated as ours, but no tenses for past, present and future. The division does not exist. What does this say about time?

Matter, that thing the most solid and the well-known, which you are holding in your hands and which makes up your body, is now known to be mostly empty space. Empty space and points of light. What does this say about the reality of the world?

MY NAME IS Jordan. This is the first thing I saw.

It was night, about a quarter to twelve, the sky divided in halves, one cloudy, the other fair. The clouds hung over the wood, there was no distance between them and the top of the trees. Where the sky was clear, over the river and the flat fields newly ploughed, the moon, almost full, shone out of a yellow aureole and reflected in the bow of the water. There were cattle in the field across, black against the slope of the hill, not moving, sleeping. One light, glittering from the only house, looked like the moat-light of a giant's castle. Tall trees flanked it. A horse ran loose in the courtyard, its hooves sparking the stone.

Then the fog came. The fog came from the river in thin spirals like spirits in a churchyard and thickened with the force of a genie from a bottle. The bulrushes were buried first, then the trunks of the trees, then the forks and the junctions. The top of the trees floated in the fog, making suspended islands for the birds.

The cattle were all drowned and the moat-light, like a lighthouse, appeared and vanished and vanished and appeared, cutting the air like a bright sword.

The fog came towards me and the sky that had been clear was covered up. It was bitterly cold, my hair was damp and I had no hand-warmer. I tried to find the path but all I found were hares with staring eyes, poised in the middle of the field and turned to stone. I began to walk with my hands stretched out in front of me, as do those troubled in sleep, and in this way, for the first time, I traced the lineaments of my own face opposite me.

Every journey conceals another journey within its lines: the path not taken and the forgotten angle. These are journeys

I wish to record. Not the ones I made, but the ones I might have made, or perhaps did make in some other place or time. I could tell you the truth as you will find it in diaries and maps and log-books. I could faithfully describe all that I saw and heard and give you a travel book. You could follow it then, tracing those travels with your finger, putting red flags where I went.

For the Greeks, the hidden life demanded invisible ink. They wrote an ordinary letter and in between the lines set out another letter, written in milk. The document looked innocent enough until one who knew better sprinkled coal-dust over it. What the letter had been no longer mattered; what mattered was the life flaring up undetected . . .
till now.

I discovered that my own life was written invisibly, was squashed between the facts, was flying without me like the Twelve Dancing Princesses who shot from their window every night and returned home every morning with torn dresses and worn-out slippers and remembered nothing.

I resolved to set a watch on myself like a jealous father, trying to catch myself disappearing through a door just noticed in the wall. I knew I was being adulterous; that what I loved was not going on at home. I was giving myself the slip and walking through this world like a shadow. The longer I eluded myself the more obsessed I became with the thought of discovery. Occasionally, in company, someone would snap their fingers in front of my face and ask, 'Where are you?' For a long time I had no idea, but gradually I began to find evidence of the other life and gradually it appeared before me.

'Remember the rock from whence ye are hewn and the pit from whence ye are digged.'

My mother carved this on a medallion and hung it round my neck the day she found me in the slime by the river. I was wrapped up in a rotting sack such as kittens are drowned in, but my head was wedged uppermost against the bank. I heard dogs coming towards me and a roar in the water and a face as round as the moon with hair falling on either side bobbed over me. She scooped me up, she tied me between her breasts whose nipples stood out like walnuts. She took

me home and kept me there with fifty dogs and no company
but her own.

I had a name but I have forgotten it.

They call me the Dog-Woman and it will do. I call him
Jordan and it will do. He has no other name before or
after. What was there to call him, fished as he was from
the stinking Thames? A child can't be called Thames, no and
not Nile either, for all his likeness to Moses. But I wanted to
give him a river name, a name not bound to anything, just
as the waters aren't bound to anything. When a woman gives
birth her waters break and she pours out the child and the
child runs free. I would have liked to pour out a child from
my body but you have to have a man for that and there's no
man who's a match for me.

When Jordan was a baby he sat on top of me much as a fly
rests on a hill of dung. And I nourished him as a hill of dung
nourishes a fly, and when he had eaten his fill he left me.

Jordan . . .

I should have named him after a stagnant pond and then
I could have kept him, but I named him after a river and in
the flood-tide he slipped away.

When Jordan was three I took him to see a great rarity and
that was my undoing. There was news that one Thomas
Johnson had got himself an edible fruit of the like never
seen in England. This Johnson, though he's been dead for
twenty years now, was a herbalist by trade, though I'd say
he was more than that. When a woman found herself too
round for her liking and showing no blood by the moon, it
was Johnson she visited with only a lantern for company.
And when she came back all flat and smiling she said it was

11

Mistletoe or Cat-nip or some such, but I say he sucked it out for the Devil.

Nevertheless, it being daylight and a crowd promised such as we see only for a dog and a bear, I took Jordan on a hound-lead and pushed my way through the gawpers and sinners until we got to the front and there was Johnson himself trying to charge money for a glimpse of the thing.

I lifted Jordan up and I told Johnson that if he didn't throw back his cloth and let us see this wonder I'd cram his face so hard into my breasts that he'd wish he'd never been suckled by a woman, so truly would I smother him.

He starts humming and hawing and reaching for some coloured jar behind his head, and I thought, he'll not let no genie out on me with its forked tongue and balls like jewels, so I grabbed him and started to push him into my dress. He was soon coughing and crying because I haven't had that dress off in five years.

'Well, then,' I said, holding him back, the way you would a weasel. 'Where is this wonder?'

'God save me,' he cried, 'a moment for my smelling salts, dear lady.'

But I would have none of it and whipped off the cover myself, and I swear that what he had resembled nothing more than the private parts of an Oriental. It was yellow and livid and long.

'It is a banana, madam,' said the rogue.

A banana? What on God's good earth was a banana?

'Such a thing never grew in Paradise,' I said.

'Indeed it did, madam,' says he, all puffed up like a poison adder. 'This fruit is from the Island of Bermuda, which is closer to Paradise than you will ever be.'

He lifted it up above his head, and the crowd, seeing it for the first time, roared and nudged each other and demanded to know what poor fool had been so reduced as to sell his vitality.

'It's either painted or infected,' said I, 'for there's none such a colour that I know.'

Johnson shouted above the din as best he could . . .

'THIS IS NOT SOME UNFORTUNATE'S RAKE. IT IS

THE FRUIT OF A TREE. IT IS TO BE PEELED AND EATEN.'

At this there was unanimous retching. There was no good woman could put that to her mouth, and for a man it was the practice of cannibals. We had not gone to church all these years and been washed in the blood of Jesus only to eat ourselves up the way the Heathen do.

I pulled on the hound-lead in order to take Jordan away, but the lead came up in my hands. I ducked down into the shuffle of bare feet and torn stockings and a gentleman's buckle here and there. He was gone. My boy was gone. I let out a great bellow such as cattle do and would have gone on bellowing till Kingdom Come had not some sinner taken my ear and turned me to look under Johnson's devilish table.

I saw Jordan standing stock still. He was standing with both his arms upraised and staring at the banana above Johnson's head. I put my head next to his head and looked where he looked and I saw deep blue waters against a pale shore and trees whose branches sang with green and birds in fairground colours and an old man in a loin-cloth.

This was the first time Jordan set sail.

London is a foul place, full of pestilence and rot. I would like to take Jordan to live in the country but we must be near Hyde Park so that I can enter my dogs in the races and fighting. Every Saturday I come home covered in saliva and bitten to death but with money in my pocket and needing nothing but a body for company.

My neighbour, who is so blackened and hairless that she has twice been mistaken for a side of salt beef wrapped in muslin, airs herself abroad as a witch. No one knows her age; what age can there be for a piece of leather like a football that serves as a head and a fantastical mass of rags that serves as a body? Not I nor anyone else has ever seen her feet beneath her skirts, so there's no knowing what it is she walks on. Her hands, always beckoning and twisting, look like the shrivelled monkeys the organ-grinders carry. She hardly moves but her hands are never still, scratching her head and her groin and darting out to snatch food and ram it square into her mouth. I'm not one for a knife and spoon myself, but I do know how to eat in company. I know how to use my bread as a plate and dollop the stew on it without spilling the lot down my dress. One look at her chin and it takes no witchery to divine what she has been eating these three weeks since. When I found Jordan, so caked in mud I could have baked him like a hedgehog, she helped me wash him down to find out what his sex was. All the time I was trying to soften his coating with a sponge of hot water she was scraping at him with her darting fingers and pulling bits off the way you would from a dog that's been hunting.

'He'll break your heart,' said she, glad to have found a mischief so close to home. 'He'll make you love him and he'll break your heart.'

Then she stopped awhile and put her ear on his chest, and the noise of his beating heart filled the room.

'There's many will want this heart but none will have it. None save one and she will spurn it.'

Then the crone almost choked herself to death on her cackles and I had to bang her on the back until she spat up some phlegm and thanked me for my pains. Truth to tell, I could have snapped her spine like a fish-bone. Had I done so, perhaps I could have changed our fate, for fate may hang on any moment and at any moment be changed. I should have killed her and found us a different story.

She crawled off into the night and I walked out after her.

I was invisible then. I, who must turn sideways through any door, can melt into the night as easily as a thin thing that sings in the choir at church. Singing is my pleasure, but not in church, for the parson said the gargoyles must remain on the outside, not seek room in the choir stalls. So I sing inside the mountain of my flesh, and my voice is as slender as a reed and my voice as no lard in it. When I sing the dogs sit quiet and people who pass in the night stop their jabbering and discontent and think of other times, when they were happy. And I sing of other times, when I was happy, though I know that these are figments of my mind and nowhere I have ever been. But

14

does it matter if the place cannot be mapped as long as I can still describe it?

One night Jordan took me sailing. We set off when the tide was high and the day was ebbing. We sailed down the Thames and out into the sea and I kept looking back and marvelling at how quickly the sights I knew best vanished. Jordan said the stars can take you anywhere. On either side low buildings hung over the water, their floors well raised on poles. Here and there the dredgers waded in between these poles, swirling the dark mass with their sticks and filling their wicker baskets with rubbish. Only a week ago one found an anchor said to have come from Rome when we were all barbarians with our hair at our waists. The dredgers have no pride and will duck into the filth for anything. It is true that one of their company lives in a fine manor house in Chelsea, but for all his elevation he and his wife and brats still resemble the waste that sustains them. She is a brown string and he is a great turd. Their children fill up the lawn like rabbit droppings. I am a sinner, and common withal, but if I had trade enough for a rope of pearls I'd wash my neck before I wore them.

Jordan told me to put on my best clothes for our voyage. I did so, and a plumed hat that sat on my head as a bird nests in a tree. He gave me a comfortable seat and asked me ten times or more whether I was warm enough. I was warm. I was seeing the world.

When it was fully dark Jordan lit lanterns round the sides of the boat. He came to me and said it was the shortest night of the year and that in a few hours the sun would be up and I would see something I'd never seen before. He wouldn't say anything else, and I racked my brains to think what flights of fancy he might have made for me. Besides, I pride myself on having seen more than most, including a mummy from Egypt. I didn't see the bandages themselves but I saw the gilded tomb as it passed through London on its way to Enstone. It was a present from good Queen Henrietta to a favourite of hers who had made a wondrous garden full of continental devices.

And I have seen a banana.

15

What, then, could Jordan have prepared?

We waited in the boat with the soft smacking on either side and Jordan told me stories of the places he'd been and the plants he'd brought back to England. He's seen all the French ways, and the Italian too, and he's been to Persia with John Tradescant. Tradescant died soon after Jordan brought the first pineapple to England, but in the years before he filled his house in Lambeth with oddities and rarities from the far ends of the earth. 'The Ark', as it pleased him to call his home, was so jammed with curiosities that a visitor might never find room to hang his hat. But the very great went there, including the King, and I have seen the King. What wonders are there left?

'Look,' said Jordan.

We were out at sea. Grey waves with white heads. A thin line in the distance where the sky dropped into the water. There were no birds, no buildings, no people and no boats. A light wind ruffled us.

Then we saw the sun. We saw the sun rising over the water, and the light got louder and louder until we were shouting to make ourselves heard, and I saw the sun on Jordan's face, and the last glimmer of lanterns, and against the final trace of the moon a flight of seagulls that came from nowhere and seemed to be born of the sun itself.

We stayed where we were in the rocking water until the night fishermen came in silent convoy. They hailed us and threw Jordan two fishes and then, looking at me, they threw him a third.

I had brought a loaf of bread, and we cooked our breakfast and left the remains to the circling gulls. Then we sailed home with the sun on our backs, and as we entered the Thames I looked behind me once. What I remember is the shining water and the size of the world.

The shining water and the size of the world.

I have seen both again and again since I left my mother on the banks of the black Thames, but in my mind it is always the same place I return to, and that one place not the most beautiful nor the most surprising.

To escape from the weight of the world, I leave my body where it is, in conversation or at dinner, and walk through a series of winding streets to a house standing back from the road.

The streets are badly lit and the distance from one side to the other no more than the span of my arms. The stone crumbles, the cobbles are uneven. The people who throng the streets shout at each other, their voices rising from the mass of heads and floating upwards towards the church spires and the great copper bells that clang the end of the day. Their words, rising up, form a thick cloud over the city, which every so often must be thoroughly cleansed of too much language. Men and women in balloons fly up from the main square and, armed with mops and scrubbing brushes, do battle with the canopy of words trapped under the sun.

The words resist erasure. The oldest and most stubborn form a thick crust of chattering rage. Cleaners have been bitten by words still quarrelling, and in one famous lawsuit a woman whose mop had been eaten and whose hand was badly mauled by a vicious row sought to bring the original antagonists to court. The men responsible made their defence on the grounds that the words no longer belonged to them. Years had passed. Was it their fault if the city had failed to deal with its overheads? The judge ruled against the plaintiff but ordered the city to buy her a new mop. She was not satisfied, and was later found lining the chimneys of her accused with vitriol.

I once accompanied a cleaner in a balloon and was amazed to hear, as the sights of the city dropped away, a faint murmuring like bees. The murmuring grew louder and louder till it sounded like the clamouring of birds, then like the deafening noise of schoolchildren let out for the holidays. She pointed with her mop and I saw a vibrating mass of many colours appear before us. We could no longer speak to each other and be heard.

She aimed her mop at a particularly noisy bright red band of words who, from what I could make out, had escaped from a group of young men on their way home from a brothel. I could see from the set of my companion's mouth that she found this particular job distasteful, but she persevered, and in a few moments all that remained was the fading pink of a few ghostly swear-words.

Next we were attacked by a cloud of wrath spewed from a parson caught fornicating his mother. The cloud wrapped round the balloon and I feared for our lives. I could not see my guide but I could hear her coughing against the noxious smell. Suddenly I was drenched in a sweet fluid and all returned to lightness.

'I have conquered them with Holy Water,' she said, showing me a stone jar marked with the Bishop's seal.

After that our task was much easier. Indeed I was sorry to see the love-sighs of young girls swept away. My companion, though she told me it was strictly forbidden, caught a sonnet in a wooden box and gave it to me as a memento. If I open the box by the tiniest amount I may hear it, repeating itself endlessly as it is destined to do until someone sets it free.

Towards the end of the day we joined with the other balloons brushing away the last few stray and vagabond words. The sky under the setting sun was the colour of veined marble, and a great peace surrounded us. As we descended through the clean air we saw, passing us by from time to time, new flocks of words coming from people in the streets who, not content with the weight of their lives, continually turned the heaviest of things into the lightest of properties.

We landed outside the university, where the dons, whose arguments had so thickly populated the ether that they had seen neither sun nor rain for the past five years, welcomed us like heroes and took us in to feast.

That night two lovers whispering under the lead canopy of the church were killed by their own passion. Their effusion of words, unable to escape through the Saturnian discipline of lead, so filled the spaces of the loft that the air was all driven away. The lovers suffocated, but when the sacristan opened the tiny door the words tumbled him over in their desire to be free, and were seen flying across the city in the shape of doves.

When Jordan was a boy he made paper boats and floated them on the river. From this he learned how the wind affects a sail, but he never learned how love affects the heart. His patience was exceeded only by his hope. He spent days and nights with his bits of wood salvaged from chicken crates, and any piece of paper he could steal became a sail. I used to watch him standing in the mud or lying face down, his nose almost in the current, his hands steadying the boat and then letting it go straight into the wind. Letting go hours of himself. When the time came he did the same with his heart. He didn't believe in shipwreck.

And he came home to me with his boats broken and his face streaked with tears, and we sat with our lamp and mended what we could, and the next day was the first day all over again. But when he lost his heart there was no one to sit with him. He was alone.

In the city of words that I have told you about the smell of wild strawberries was the smell characteristic of the house that I have not yet told you about. The runners of these plants spread from the beds bounded by stone tiles and fastened themselves over terracotta pots and flaking ironwork and hid the big flags that paved the courtyard. Anyone coming to the outer gate would find themselves confronted by waves of green dotted underneath with tiny red berries, some clutched in spiders' webs like forgotten rubies. There was a way through to an oaked door, and beyond the door the square hall of the house with other doors leading off it. There were four suits of armour in the hall, and a mace.

The family who lived in the house were dedicated to a strange custom. Not one of them would allow their feet to touch the floor. Open the doors off the hall and you will see, not floors, but bottomless pits. The furniture of the house is suspended on racks from the ceiling; the dining table supported by great chains, each link six inches thick. To dine here is a great curiosity, for the visitor must sit in a gilded chair and allow himself to be winched up to join his place setting. He comes last, the householders already seated and making merry, swinging their feet over the abyss where crocodiles live. Everyone who dines has a multiplicity of glasses and cutlery lest some should be dropped accidentally. Whatever food is left over at the end of the meal is scraped into the pit, from whence a fearful crunching can be heard.

When everyone has eaten their fill, the gentlemen remain at the table and the ladies walk in order of precedence across a tightrope to another room, where they may have biscuits and wine with water.

It is well known that the ceiling of one room is the floor of another, but the household ignores this ever-downward necessity and continues ever upward, celebrating ceilings but denying floors, and so their house never ends and they must travel by winch or rope from room to room, calling to one another as they go.

The house is empty now, but it was there, dangling over dinner, illuminated by conversation and rich in the juices of a wild duck, that I noticed a woman whose face was a sea voyage I had not the courage to attempt.

I did not speak to her, though I spoke to all the rest, and at midnight she put on flat pumps and balanced the yards of rope without faltering. She was a dancer.

I spent the night in my suspended bed and slept badly. At dawn I was leaning out of the window, a rope round my waist. The moon was still visible: it seemed to me that I was closer to the moon than to the ground. A cold wind numbed my ears.

Then I saw her. She was climbing down from her window on a thin rope which she cut and re-knotted a number of times during the descent. I strained my eyes to follow her, but she was gone.

It must have been in about 1640, when Jordan was something close to ten, that he met John Tradescant on the banks of the boiling Thames. It was a summer so hot that a housewife never had to lay a fire for her roasted pig; all she need do was tether it in the yard for an hour. For myself, the wafts of heat regularly assaulting me seemed to come from the very doors of Hell, and I am sure that on Judgement Day those who are not on the side of the angels will feel this same scorching on their faces and toes as a foretaste of their torments to come. I could scarcely step outside without sweating off me enough liquid to fill a bucket. These waterfalls took with them countless lice and other timid creatures, and being forced to put myself often under the pump I can truly say I was clean.

'Cleanliness is next to Godliness,' said a Puritan passing by.

'God looks on the heart, not a poor woman's dress,' I retorted, but there was no stopping his little sermon, which he gave with his eyes rolled back as piously as a rabbit's.

It is true that the ferment in the city is due not only to the heat, but also to the King seeming to turn Papish on us, and Parliament being in uproar, and Cromwell with his lump-shaped head stirring it and stirring it.

Jordan had got up early one morning to sail his boats and I had promised him an apple after my duties with the dogs. Squinting against the light I set off to find him and saw him in the distance sitting on an eaten-up jetty, a gentleman beside him. I hurried myself, thinking it might be some smooth-faced rascal set to chivvy him away.

As I got closer Jordan waved to me and the gentleman stood up and bowed slightly, which pleased me a good deal, and said his name was John Tradescant. Then he gave a little pause and said, 'Gardener to the King.'

He was a good-looking man in his thirties, and he gave no sign of fear that the wormy jetty might dissolve at any moment, with my weight swaying it as a crow would a wren's house. He asked if I cared to sit down, and I took pity on him and trod back onto the bank. He squatted a while to fiddle in his bag and came out with three peaches. One he offered me, and one he gave to Jordan, who held it in both hands as though it were a crystal ball.

'I grew them,' said Tradescant. 'You are eating from the King's tree.'

And then he bit into his and spurted the juice right over himself. Cautiously I bit into mine, but in a more ladylike fashion. Jordan did nothing, and I had to remind him of his manners.

Tradescant told me he had been walking the length of the river from Putney to Mermaid Dock, troubling himself with a problem. He had seen a little boat sail by and was so enchanted by its easy passage that he forgot his melancholy

22

and relived in his mind his own days of adventure on the seas. For years, until 1637 when his father died, he had sailed to exotic places collecting such rare plants as mortals had ever seen. These he housed in his father's museum and physic garden at Lambeth. On his father's death he was forced to return from voyaging in Virginia and take up the family post of gardener to the King. He liked it well enough, but sometimes he felt hollow inside, and on those days he knew his heart was at sea.

'A man must have responsibilities,' he said. 'But they are not always the ones he would choose.'

'Indeed not,' said I, 'and for a woman the Devil's burden is twice the load.'

As Tradescant had stood on the bank watching the boat, his body like stone, his mind racing, Jordan had come running by, shouting encouragement to his little ship. His eyes were for his business, not on Tradescant's thighs, and in a moment the two of them were flat down on the bank and Jordan was torn between the terror of being walloped and the possibility of losing his boat. As it was, Tradescant hauled him up, rescued the vessel and took the two of them to sit down on the jetty, where I found them.

He showed Jordan how to lengthen the rudder so that the boat could sail in deeper water without capsizing. He told him stories of rocks sprung out of the ocean, the only land as far as the eye could see, and no life on that land but screaming birds. He said that the sea is so vast no one will ever finish sailing it. That every mapped-out journey contains another journey hidden in its lines . . .

I pooh-poohed this, for the earth is surely a manageable place made of blood and stone and entirely flat. I believe I could walk from one side to the other, had I the inclination. And if a great body of us had the inclination there would be no part of the earth left untouched. What then of journeys folded in on themselves like a concertina?

But Jordan believed him, and when Tradescant left Jordan and I went home, he skipping ahead and carrying his ship and I a few steps behind. I watched his thin body and black hair and wondered how long it would be before he made his ships too big to carry, and then one of them would carry him and leave me behind for ever.

How hideous am I?

My nose is flat, my eyebrows are heavy. I have only a few teeth and those are a poor show, being black and broken. I had smallpox when I was a girl and the caves in my face are home enough for fleas. But I have fine blue eyes that see in the dark. As for my size, I know only that before Jordan was found a travelling circus came through Cheapside, and in that circus was an elephant. We were all pleased to see the elephant, a huge beast with a wandering nose. Its trick was to sit itself in a seat like any well-bred gentleman, and wear an eyeglass. There was a seat on its opposite side, and a guessing game was to offer up a certain number of persons to climb on to the other seat, topsyturvy, as best they could, and outweigh Samson, as the elephant was named. No one had succeeded, though the prize was a vat of ale.

One night, pushing along with a ribbon in my hair, I thought to try and outweigh Samson myself. I had taken a look at him and he seemed none too big for me. So I got hold of the man who was bawling and jeering at the crowd to pit themselves against a mere beast and said I would take the seat.

'But, madam,' screeched the little bit of vermin, 'I see you weigh no more than an angel.'

'You know nothing of the Scriptures,' said I. 'For nowhere in the Holy Book is there anything to be said about the weight of an angel.'

His eyebrows shot up to Heaven, the only part of him ever likely to get there, and he started banging his drum and bellowing like one at a funeral, saying here was a sight and gather round and gather round. Soon I could hardly breathe for the heat coming off the bodies, and the elephant itself had to be revived with a bucket of cold water.

'Let me lead you to the chair,' said the knock-kneed knave, the bells on his hat winking and tinkling.

I am gracious by nature and I allowed myself to be led.

'I will have to search you,' said the creature, rolling his eyes at the crowd. 'I must be sure that you are free of lead weights and any other advantages.'

'Touch me you won't,' I cried. 'I'll show you what there is.' And I lifted up my dress over my head. I was wearing no underclothes in respect of the heat.

There was a great swooning amongst the crowd, and I heard a voice compare me to a mountain range. However, it silenced my Lord Fool, who made no more remarks about a search and simply showed me the chair.

I took a deep breath, filling my lungs with air, and threw myself at the seat with all my might. There was a roar from round about me. I opened my eyes and looked towards Samson. He had vanished. His chair swung empty like a summer-house seat, his eyeglass lay in the bottom. I looked higher, following the gaze of the people. Far above us, far far away like a black star in a white sky, was Samson.

It is a responsibility for a woman to have forced an elephant into the sky. What it says of my size I cannot tell, for an elephant looks big, but how am I to know what it weighs? A balloon looks big and weighs nothing.

I know that people are afraid of me, either for the yapping of my dogs or because I stand taller than any of them. When I was a child my father swung me up on to his knees to tell a story and I broke both his legs. He never touched me again, except with the point of the whip he used for the dogs. But my mother, who lived only a while and was so light that she dared not go out in a wind, could swing me on her back and carry me for miles. There was talk of witchcraft but what is stronger than love?

When Jordan was new I sat him on the palm of my hand the way I would a puppy, and I held him to my face and let him pick the fleas out of my scars.

25

He was always happy. We were happy together, and if he noticed that I am bigger than most he never mentioned it. He was proud of me because no other child had a mother who could hold a dozen oranges in her mouth at once.

How hideous am I?

One morning, soon after the start of the Civil War that should have been over in a month and lasted eight years, Tradescant came to our house looking for Jordan. I was shouting at a neighbour of mine, a sunken block of a fellow with slant eyes and a nose to hang a hat on. This cranesbill was telling me that the King was wrong to make war on his own people, and I was telling him that if the foul-mouthed Scots hadn't started their jiggery-pokery again, always wanting a fight with someone, we'd have had no war. We'd lived with a King and without a Parliament for eleven years, and now we'd got a Parliament and precious little of a King.

As far as I know it, and I have only a little learning, the King had been forced to call a Parliament to grant him money for his war against the kilted beasts and their savage ways. Savage to the core, and the poor King trying only to make them use a proper prayer book. They wouldn't have his prayer book and in a most unchristian manner threatened his throne. The King, turning to his own people, found himself with a Parliament full of Puritans who wouldn't grant him money until he had granted them reform. Not content with the Church of England that good King Henry had bequeathed to us all, they wanted what they called 'A Church of God'.

They said that the King was a wanton spendthrift, that the bishops were corrupt, that our Book of Common Prayer was full of Popish ways, that the Queen herself, being French, was bound to be full of Popish ways. Oh they hated everything that was grand and fine and full of life, and they went about in their flat grey suits with their flat grey faces poking out the top. The only thing fancy about them was their handkerchiefs, which they liked to be trimmed with lace and kept as white as they reckoned their souls to be. I've seen Puritans going past a theatre where all was merriment and pleasure and holding

26

their starched linen to their noses for fear they might smell pleasure and be infected by it.

It didn't take them long to close down every theatre in London once they got a bit of power.

But didn't our Saviour turn the water into wine?

Our own minister of God soon turned Puritan and started denouncing the King from his pulpit.

'Preacher Scroggs,' I said, one morning after he had delivered his sermon on the text 'And the memory of the wicked shall rot', 'do you not know that our King is so by Divine Right?'

He fixed me with the better of his two squint eyes and clasped his hands together.

'Look to the Heavenly King, lady,' he said. 'There is no earthly power but Satan.'

I heard from his wife that he makes love to her through a hole in the sheet.

'Does he not kiss you?' I said.

'He has never kissed me,' she answered, 'for fear of lust.'

Then lust must be a powerful thing, if to kiss her that most resembles a hare, with great ears and staring eyes, brings it on.

It is a true saying, that what you fear you find.

My neighbour, who has a fondness for Preacher Scroggs, largely since like finds like, was addressing me in the most pompous terms about the Will of God, as though he knew God as well as I do my dogs. Thus I was forced to shout him down, reason being wasted on a block, and thus did Tradescant find me.

'Madam, madam, calm yourself,' he said in his gentle way.

I turned, and though I hadn't seen him for two years I recognized him at once.

'Mr Tradescant,' I said, 'I am defending the King.'

'A noble cause,' said he.

At this my neighbour claimed he'd never kneel before a king until he knelt before Jesus. Any time now, he said, the Rule of Saints would begin on earth and all the sinners would be burned up and confounded.

I had no choice but to strangle him, and though I used only one hand and held him from the ground at arm's length, he was purple in no time and poor John Tradescant was swinging on my arm like a little monkey, begging me to stop.

'I'll spare him for your sake, sir,' I said, and dropped the ugly thing into his own midden.

I thought no more of him but took Tradescant into our house for a pot of ale. He seemed pale, no doubt from his journey.

'I've come about Jordan,' he said.

And it seemed that he wanted a gardener's boy at Wimbledon where he was laying out a great garden for Queen Henrietta. He refused to let the troubles interrupt his work. He had it in his mind that when the Queen returned from the Continent in triumph to the King, bringing the children who were hidden for safety, the garden would stand as a monument to her courage.

But how could I lose Jordan, so dear to me and my only comfort?

Tradescant tried all his gentle ways to persuade me. I continued to refuse, saying it was too far for my boy to travel daily. And yet I wanted Jordan to have the work, knowing how it would delight him to see such exotic things growing all in one place. At length I hit on a solution.

'I'll accompany him,' I said.

Tradescant seemed surprised, so I continued.

'I have a mind to take the air of Wimbledon for a time.'

'There's nowhere for you to live,' he said. 'Jordan will have to share with the other men of the estate.'

I have a flair for architecture, having built my own hut, and I assured Tradescant that I could build another.

He spread his hands, he sighed, but I knew I had beaten him.

'And my hounds, I must bring them.'

He asked me how many I had, and I comforted him that there were just a few at present.

'When can I expect you?'

'We will begin our journey tomorrow. In what direction is Wimbledon?'

He said the coachman would be sure to know, and as he

seemed in a hurry to leave I did not press him, thinking I could find out from the innkeeper at the Crown of Thorns.

It was three days later that a half-wit went foaming and stuttering to Mr Tradescant, crying that the garden had been invaded by an evil spirit and her Hounds of Hell. Tradescant came running to the great gates, and he must have been relieved to see it was only myself holding Jordan by the hand.

'Your dogs,' he said, and I saw his Adam's apple bobbing up and down.

'Yes,' I replied, 'no more than thirty and only five ready for breeding.'

He was a gentleman, and if he had seemed taken aback he soon recovered himself and asked if he might pay for our carriage and perhaps send help to fetch our belongings.

'There is no carriage,' I told him, 'and here are our belongings.'

I raised a bundle of red cloth like a great Christmas pudding. Jordan had his boat under his arm.

'But how . . . ?'

'We walked,' I said. 'And when Jordan was tired I carried him.'

Tradescant said nothing, but tried to take my bundle, which immediately flattened him to the ground. Very tenderly, as a mother knows how, I scooped him up in my arms, the bundle on top of him, and with my thirty dogs and Jordan coming behind we entered the gate of the great house and began our new life as servants of the King.

I slept in my suspended bed for two fitful hours and then winched myself down to breakfast feeling sea-sick.

My hosts that morning were engaged in archery practice

and I was able to excuse myself and comb the city for the dancer. No one in the house recalled her, though how that were possible with her loveliness that devoured the rest of the company in tongues of flame I do not know.

I began first at the theatre and then went on to the opera and then with increasing dread in ever-decreasing circles of infamy: cafés and casinos and bawdy-houses and at last to a pen of prostitutes kept by a rich man for his friends. The women were gracious but urged me to return in female disguise. That way I might be granted admittance. As a man, however chaste, I would be driven away or made a eunuch.

I did as they advised and came to them in a simple costume hired for the day. They praised my outfit and made me blush by stroking my cheek and commenting on its smoothness.

We drank unfortified wine, and when the custodian passed and asked who it was they were entertaining one stood up and said I was her cousin from afar.

They knew nothing of the dancer. She was not of their company, though they promised to enquire among friends.

How could they bear such privation?'

Their quarters were very comfortable, with every kind of couch and bed and game to play, but they were not allowed to go outside.

How could they live without space?

There was silence, and it seemed as though they were communicating without words. Then one spoke to me and explained that they were not so confined as it seemed. That through the night they came and went as they pleased.

How could this be? The house was barred. Each door had thirteen locks. The windows were too high to reach and the skylights, though always kept open, could not be broached.

Underneath the house was a stream. The stream, on its way to the river on its way to the sea, passed beneath the lodgings of quite a different set of women. Nuns. This convent, the Convent of the Holy Mother, had its cellars opening over the stream. Every night, any of the women who wished to amuse herself in the city, visit friends, eat dinner with her beloved, dropped herself into the fast-flowing water and was carried downstream towards the convent. It was the custom of the nuns to keep watch over the stream through the night, and any of the women shooting past the convent vault was immediately fished out in a great shrimping net by the nun on duty.

Some of the women had lovers in the convent; others, keeping a change of clothes there, went their way in the outside world. At dawn the women were let down into the water, and with great fortitude swam upstream into their locked citadel.

Their owner, being a short-sighted man of scant intelligence, never noticed that the women under his care were always different. There was an unspoken agreement in the city that any woman who wanted to amass a fortune quickly would go and work in the house and rob the clients and steal the ornaments supposedly safe on the wall. He did not know it but this selfish man, to whom life was just another commodity, had financed the futures of thousands of women, who were now across the world or trading in shops or as merchants. He had also, singlehanded, paid for the convent's renowned stock of fine wine and any number of alterpieces.

Some years later I heard that he had come into his pleasure chamber one day and found it absolutely empty of women and of treasures. He never fathomed the matter and made no connection between that event and the sudden increase in novitiates at the Convent of the Holy Mother.

I have met a number of people who, anxious to be free of the burdens of their gender, have dressed themselves men as women and women as men.

After my experience in the pen of prostitutes I decided to continue as a woman for a time and took a job on a fish stall.

I noticed that women have a private language. A language not dependent on the constructions of men but structured by signs and expressions, and that uses ordinary words as code-words meaning something other.

In my petticoats I was a traveller in a foreign country. I did not speak the language. I was regarded with suspicion.

I watched women flirting with men, pleasing men, doing

business with men, and then I watched them collapsing into laughter, sharing the joke, while the men, all unknowing, felt themselves master of the situation and went off to brag in barrooms and to preach from pulpits the folly of the weaker sex.

This conspiracy of women shocked me. I like women; I am shy of them but I regard them highly. I never guessed how much they hate us or how deeply they pity us. They think we are children with too much pocket money. The woman who owned the fish stall warned me never to try and cheat another woman but always to try and charge the men double or send them away with a bad catch.

'Their noses are dull,' she said. 'They won't be able to mark a day-old lobster from a fresh one.'

And she asked me to remember that a woman, if cheated, will never forget and will some day pay you back, even if it takes years, while a man will rave and roar and slap you perhaps and then be distracted by some other thing.

Thinking to teach me about men, worrying that I knew nothing, she wrote me a rule book of which I will list the first page.

1. Men are easy to please but are not pleased for long before some new novelty must delight them.
2. Men are easy to make passionate but are unable to sustain it.
3. Men are always seeking soft women but find their lives in ruins without strong women.
4. Men must be occupied at all times otherwise they make mischief.
5. Men deem themselves weighty and women light. Therefore it is simple to tie a stone round their necks and drown them should they become too troublesome.
6. Men are best left in groups by themselves where they will entirely wear themselves out in drunkenness and competition. While this is taking place a woman may carry on with her own life unhindered.
7. Men are never never to be trusted with what is closest to your heart, and if it is they who are closest to your heart, do not tell them.

8. If a man asks you for money, do not give it to him.
9. If you ask a man for money and he does not give it to you, sell his richest possession and leave at once.
10. Your greatest strength is that every man believes he knows the sum and possibility of every woman.

I was much upset when I read this first page, but observing my own heart and the behaviour of those around me I conceded it to be true. Then my heaviness was at its limit and I could not raise myself up from where I was sitting. But I did look around me and I saw that I was one in a long line of unfortunates sitting like crows on a fallen tree. All were wailing piteously and none could move on account of their sorrows.

I was lucky that my hands were free, and reaching down into my fish basket I took out a red mullet and waved it over my head.

Soon a flock of sea birds appeared screeching at the sight of the fish. I waved another in my left hand, and as I had hoped the birds dived to catch the fish.

When they fastened their beaks on to my bait I did not let go and the birds, maddened at any resistance to their feeding, flapped all the harder and succeeded in pulling me up with them. I let go at once, but the birds, somehow imagining me as a great fish, carried me up into the air and flew me over the city and out to sea.

Far below I watched the waves crashing against high cliffs and saw the sails of ships passing to the Tropics. I fainted from fear, and when I revived I was no longer in the air but seemed to be on the windowsill of a well-appointed house in a town I did not recognize. A young girl came to the window and, asking me if I were the sister she had prayed for, courteously invited me to bed with her, where I passed the night in some confusion.

What is love?

On the morning after our arrival at Wimbledon I awoke in a pool of philosophic thought, though comforted by Jordan's regular breathing and the snorts of my thirty dogs.

I am too huge for love. No one, male or female, has ever dared to approach me. They are afraid to scale mountains.

I wonder about love because the parson says that only God can truly love us and the rest is lust and selfishness.

In church, there are carvings of a man with his member swollen out like a marrow, rutting a woman whose teats swish the ground like a cow before milking. She has her eyes closed and he looks up to Heaven, and neither of them notice the grass is on fire.

The parson had these carvings done especially so that we could contemplate our sin and where it must lead.

There are women too, hot with lust, their mouths sucking at each other, and men grasping one another the way you would a cattle prod.

We file past every Sunday to humble ourselves and stay clean for another week, but I have noticed a bulge here and there where all should be quiet and God-like.

For myself, the love I've known has come from my dogs, who care nothing for how I look, and from Jordan, who says that though I am as wide and muddy as the river that is his namesake, so am I too his kin. As for the rest of this sinning world, they treat me well enough for my knowledge and pass me by when they can.

I breed boarhounds as my father did before me and as I hoped Jordan would do after me. But he would not stay. His head was stuffed with stories of other continents where men have their faces in their chests and some hop on one foot defying the weight of nature.

These hoppers cover a mile at a bound and desire no sustenance other than tree-bark. It is well known that their companions are serpents, the very beast that drove us all from Paradise and makes us still to sin. These beasts are so wily that if they hear the notes of a snake-charmer they lay one ear to the earth and stopper up the other with their tails. Would I could save myself from sin by stoppering up my ears with a tail or any manner of thing.

I am a sinner, not in body but in mind. I know what love sounds like because I have heard it through the wall, but I do not know what it feels like. What can it be like, two bodies slippery as eels on a mud-flat, panting like dogs after a pig?

I fell in love once, if love be that cruelty which takes us straight to the gates of Paradise only to remind us they are closed for ever.

There was a boy who used to come by with a coatful of things to sell. Beads and ribbons hung on the inside and his pockets were crammed with fruit knives and handkerchiefs and buckles and bright thread. He had a face that made me glad.

I used to get up an hour early and comb my hair, which normally I would do only at Christmas-time in honour of our Saviour. I decked myself in my best clothes like a bullock at a fair, but none of this made him notice me and I felt my heart shrivel to the size of a pea. Whenever he turned his back to leave I always stretched out my hand to hold him a moment, but his shoulder-blades were too sharp to touch. I drew his image in the dirt by my bed and named all my mother's chickens after him.

Eventually I decided that true love must be clean love and I boiled myself a cake of soap . . .

I hate to wash, for it exposes the skin to contamination. I follow the habit of King James, who only ever washed his fingertips and yet was pure in heart enough to give us the Bible in good English.

I hate to wash, but knowing it to be a symptom of love I was not surprised to find myself creeping towards the pump in the dead of night like a ghoul to a tomb. I had determined to cleanse all of my clothes, my underclothes and myself. I did this in one passage by plying at the pump handle, first with my right arm and washing my left self, then with my left arm and washing my right self. When I was so drenched that to wring any part of me left a puddle at my feet I waited outside the baker's until she began her work and sat myself by the ovens until morning. I had a white coating from the flour, but that served to make my swarthy skin more fair.

In this new state I presented myself to my loved one, who graced me with all of his teeth at once and swore that if only he could reach my mouth he would kiss me there and then. I swept him from his feet and said, 'Kiss me now,' and closed my eyes for the delight. I kept them closed for some five minutes and then, opening them to see what had happened, I saw that he had fainted dead away. I carried him to the pump that had last seen my devotion and doused him good and hard, until he came to, wriggling like a trapped fox, and begged me let him down.

'What is it?' I cried. 'Is it love for me that affects you so?'

'No,' he said. 'It is terror.'

I saw him a few months later in another part of town with a pretty jade on his arm and his face as bright as ever.

In the morning the young girl, whose name was Zillah, told me she had been locked in this tower since her birth.

'This is not a tower,' I said. 'It is a house of some stature but nothing more.'

'No,' she said. 'You are mistaken. Go to the window.'

I did as she asked, and looked down a few feet over a street setting up for market. Women in leather aprons were piling radishes on wooden stalls, a priest was blessing a cargo of Holy Relics, while a saintly man, come early, was arguing over the price of a rib.

It was a fine morning; the air smelt of lemons.

As I looked down a stallholder turned his face and stared directly at me. I waved and smiled but he gave no sign of recognition. It did not trouble me; people are nervous of strangers.

'Is is not terrifying?' said Zillah.

Then I knew she must be having a game with me and I went and pulled her to the window.

'Come and see this steeple of radishes.'

She was silent. I noticed how pale her face was, and that her eyes were unnaturally bright. I leaned over to point out anything that might please her but the words stuck to the roof of my mouth. She was gazing down. I followed her gaze, down and further down. We were at the top of a sheer-built tower. The stone cylinder fell without relief to a platform of bitter rocks smashed by foaming waves. The coastline winding away was desolate of living things. No hut or sheepfold broke the line of tangled rosemary bushes. There was nothing but the wind and the slate-blue sea.

She pulled away from me and went to sit down on the bed. With my back to the window I asked her what it was that kept her here.

'It is myself,' she said. 'Only myself.'

It was then I realized the room had no door.

'Is there anything for me to eat?' I asked her.

She smiled, leaned under the bed and pulled out two rats by their tails.

She laughed, and walked towards me, the rats in each hand. Her eyes were clouding over, her eyes were disappearing. I could smell her breath like cheese in muslin.

I did not think of my life; I somersaulted out of the window and landed straight in the pile of radishes.

The woman in the leather apron hit me over the head, but someone behind her, pulling her off, took me by the shoulders and urged me to tell him where I had come from so suddenly.

'From the tower,' I said, pointing upwards.

The market stopped its bustle and all fell to the ground and made the sign of the cross. The purveyor of Holy Relics hung a set of martyr's teeth round his neck and sprinkled me with the dust of St Anthony.

The story was a terrible one.

A young girl caught incestuously with her sister was condemned to build her own death tower. To prolong her life she built it as high as she could, winding round and round with the stones in an endless stairway. When there were no stones left she sealed the room and the village, driven mad by her death cries, evacuated to a far-off spot where no one could hear her. Many years later the tower had been demolished by a foreigner who had built the house I saw in its place. Slowly the village had returned, but not the foreigner, nor anyone else, could live in the house. At night the cries were too loud.

The villagers were kind to me, and I helped them through the day with their stalls of exotic fruit and speckled fish, and at night the men filled their pipes and sat on the sea wall and asked me where I had come from, and why.

I did not tell them the strange means of my arrival, but I explained the destination of my heart.

'The world is full of dancers,' said one, blowing the smoke in circles round my head.

'And you have seen this one only by night,' said another.

'And escaping down a wall,' said his wife, who was scraping crabmeat into a pot.

The philosopher of the village warned me that love is better ignored than explored, for it is easier to track a barnacle goose than to follow the trajectories of the heart.

There followed a discourse on love, some of which I will reveal to you.

On the one side there were those who claimed that love, if it be allowed at all, must be kept tame by marriage vows and family ties so that its fiery heat warms the hearth but does not burn down the house.

On the other there were those who believed that only passion freed the soul from its mud-hut, and that only by loosing the heart like a coursing hare and following it until sundown could a man or woman sleep quietly at night.

The school of heaviness, who would tie down love, took

as their examples those passages of ancient literature which promise that those driven by desire, the lightest of things, suffer under weights they cannot bear. Weights far more terrible than to accept from the start that passion must spend its life in chains.

What of the woman who finds herself turning into a lotus tree as she flees her ardent lover? Her feet are rooted to the earth, soft bark creeps up her legs and little by little enfolds her groin. When she tries to tear her hair her hands are full of leaves.

What of Orpheus, who pursues his passion through the gates of Hell, only to fail at the last moment and to lose the common presence of his beloved?

And Actaeon, whose desire for Artemis turns him into a stag and leaves him torn to pieces by his own dogs?

These things are so, and may be laid out in a solemn frieze to run round the edges of the world.

Then I stood up and reminded the company of Penelope, who through her love for one man refused the easy compromise of a gilded kingdom and unravelled by night the woven weight of a day's work to leave her hands empty again in the morning.

And of Sappho, who rather than lose her lover to a man flung herself from the windy cliffs and turned her body into a bird.

It is well known that those in the grip of heavy enchantments can be wakened only by a lover's touch. Those who seem dead, who are already returning to the earth, can be restored to life, quickened again by one who is warm.

Then, it being night, and the twin stars of Castor and Pollux just visible in the sky, I spoke of that tragedy, of two brothers whose love we might find unnatural, so stricken in grief when one was killed that the other, begging for his life again, accepted instead that for half the year one might live, and for the rest of the year the other, but never the two together. So it is for us, who while on earth in these suits of lead sense the presence of one we love, not far away but too far to touch.

The villagers were silent and one by one began to move away, each in their own thoughts. A woman brushed my hair back with her hand. I stayed where I was with my shoulders against the rough sea wall and asked myself what I hadn't asked the others.

Was I searching for a dancer whose name I did not know or was I searching for the dancing part of myself?

Night.

In the dark and in the water I weigh nothing at all. I have no vanity but I would enjoy the consolation of a lover's face. After my only excursion into love I resolved never to make a fool of myself again. I was offered a job in a whore-house but I turned it down on account of my frailty of heart. Surely such to-ing and fro-ing as must go on night and day weakens the heart and inclines it to love? Not directly, you understand, but indirectly, for lust without romantic matter must be wearisome after a time. I asked a girl at the Spitalfields house about it and she told me she hates her lovers-by-the-hour but still longs for someone to come in a coach and feed her on mince-pies.

Where do they come from, these insubstantial dreams?

As for Jordan, he has not my common sense and will no doubt follow his dreams to the end of the world and then fall straight off.

I cannot school him in love, having no experience, but I can school him in its lack and perhaps persuade him that there are worse things than loneliness.

A man accosted me on our way to Wimbledon and asked me if I should like to see him.

'I see you well enough, sir,' I replied.

'Not all of me,' said he, and unbuttoned himself to show a thing much like a pea-pod.

'Touch it and it will grow,' he assured me. I did so, and indeed it did grow to look more like a cucumber.

'Wondrous, wondrous, wondrous,' he swooned, though I could see no good reason for swooning.

'Put it in your mouth,' he said. 'Yes, as you would a delicious thing to eat.'

I like to broaden my mind when I can and I did as he suggested, swallowing it up entirely and biting it off with a snap.

As I did so my eager fellow increased his swooning to the point of fainting away, and I, feeling both astonished by his rapture and disgusted by the leathery thing filling up my mouth, spat out what I had not eaten and gave it to one of my dogs.

The whore from Spitalfields had told me that men like to be consumed in the mouth, but it still seems to me a reckless act, for the member must take some time to grow again. None the less their bodies are their own, and I who know nothing of them must take instruction humbly, and if a man asks me to do the same again I'm sure I shall, though for myself I felt nothing.

In copulation, an act where the woman has a more pleasurable part, the member comes away in the great tunnel and creeps into the womb where it splits open after a time like a runner bean and deposits a little mannikin to grow in the rich soil. At least, so I am told by women who have become pregnant and must know their husbands' members as well as I do my own dogs.

When Jordan is older I will tell him what I know about the human body and urge him to be careful of his member. And yet it is not that part of him I fear for; it is his heart. His heart.

Here at Wimbledon we have a French gardener named André Mollet who has come specially to teach Tradescant the French ways with water fountains and parterres.

Like most Frenchmen he is more interested in his member than in his spade and has made amorous overtures to every woman on the estate, with the exception of myself. In honour of his tirelessness we are to have a stream shooting nine feet high with a silver ball balanced on the top. The cascading torrent will mingle with a wall of water like a hedge, dividing the fish-ponds from the peasantry.

The fish-ponds are circles and squares filled with rare waters, sometimes salt, sometimes still, containing fabulous fishes of the kind imagined but never seen.

In the largest pond are a shoal of flying fish that toss their glittering bodies in one leap from one side to the other. Do they dream of tree-tops buffeted by the wind?

In another, a curious pool shining with its own radiance from a holy well in the East, are a group of spotted toads notable for their singing. These toads do not croak, but engage in madrigals and set up an anthem more fair than any choir in church. Even the palace of the Sun King in France has nothing so rare and wonderful, though I am told he has a dancing weasel given in exchange for a hundred pear trees. For myself I prefer the running stream that leads from the bank planted with cherry and makes a basin in the grotto with the statue of the hermit. The stream is shallow, its bottom crowded with tiny pebbles, its sides sprouting watercress. Underneath the stones are fresh-water shrimps feeding on creatures even smaller than themselves. There is a rock near to its source and I very often hide behind it at evening, singing songs of love and death and waiting for the sun to set. When the orange bar is straight across the horizon the kingfisher comes with blue wings beating and dives in one swift streak. Ascends like a saint, vertical and glorious, its beak crammed with shrimp.

At sea and away from home in a creaking boat, with Tradescant sleeping beside me, there is a town I sometimes dream about, whose inhabitants are so cunning that to escape the insistence of creditors they knock down their houses in a single night and rebuild them elsewhere. So the number of buildings in the city is always constant but they are never in the same place from one day to the next.

42

For close families, and most of the people in the city are close families, this presents no problem, and it is more usual than not for the escapees to find their pursuers waiting for them on the new site of their choice.

As a subterfuge, then, it has little to recommend it, but as a game it is a most fulfilling pastime and accounts for the extraordinary longevity of the men and women who live there. We were all nomads once, and crossed the deserts and the seas on tracks that could not be detected, but were clear to those who knew the way. Since settling down and rooting like trees, but without the ability to make use of the wind to scatter our seed, we have found only infection and discontent.

In the city the inhabitants have reconciled two discordant desires: to remain in one place and to leave it behind for ever.

On arriving there for the first time I made friends with a family, and after dinner promised to call the next day. They urged me to do so, and I did, and was upset to find that the little house had been replaced by a Museum of Antiquities. The curator was sympathetic and pointed me in the right direction. I had it in mind to go back to the museum and look at the skeleton of an extinct whale. It seemed unlikely to me that a public building would feel the same need to escape as an ordinary individual.

I was mistaken. The museum had gone back to its original site by the docks, and in its place, with room to spare, was a windmill. As I watched the blades churning the air and wondered what kind of an element air must be, to seem like nothing and yet put up such resistance, the miller came to his round window and yelled something I couldn't hear. I caught hold of one of the blades as it passed by me and swung myself up beside him.

He asked me if I knew the story of the Twelve Dancing Princesses. I said I had heard it, and he told me they were still living just down the road, though of course they were quite a bit older now. Why didn't I go and see them?

Thinking that one dancer might well know another and that a dozen of them must surely know one I took a catch of herrings as a gift and banged on their door.

THE STORY OF
THE TWELVE DANCING
PRINCESSES

I BANGED ON the door and heard a voice behind me asking my name.

'My name is Jordan,' I said, though not knowing to whom.

'Down here.'

There was a well by the door with a frayed rope and a rusty bucket.

'Are you looking for me?'

I explained to the head now poking over the edge of the well that I had come to pay my respects to the Twelve Dancing Princesses.

'You can start here then,' said the head. 'I am the eldest.'

Timidly, for I have a fear of confined spaces, I swung over the edge and climbed down a wooden ladder. I found myself in a circular room, well furnished, with a silver jug coming to the boil with fresh coffee.

'I've brought you some herrings,' I said, awkwardly.

At the word 'herring' there was a sound of great delight and a hand came over my shoulder and took the whole parcel.

'Please excuse her,' said the princess. 'She is a mermaid.'

Already the mermaid, who was very beautiful but without fine graces, was gobbling the fish, dropping them back into her throat the way you or I would an oyster.

'It is the penalty of love,' sighed the princess, and began at once to tell me the story of her life.

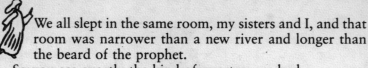We all slept in the same room, my sisters and I, and that room was narrower than a new river and longer than the beard of the prophet.

So you see exactly the kind of quarters we had.

We slept in white beds with white sheets and the moon shone through the window and made white shadows on the floor.

From this room, every night, we flew to a silver city where no one ate or drank. The occupation of the people was to dance. We wore out our dresses and slippers dancing, but because we were always sound asleep when our father came to wake us in the morning it was impossible to fathom where we had been or how.

You know that eventually a clever prince caught us flying through the window. We had given him a sleeping draught but he only pretended to drink it. He had eleven brothers and we were all given in marriage, one to each brother, and as it says lived happily ever after. We did, but not with our husbands.

I have always enjoyed swimming, and it was in deep waters one day that I came to a coral cave and saw a mermaid combing her hair. I fell in love with her at once, and after a few months of illicit meetings, my husband complaining all the time that I stank of fish, I ran away and began housekeeping with her in perfect salty bliss.

For some years I did not hear from my sisters, and then, by a strange eventuality, I discovered that we had all, in one way or another, parted from the glorious princes and were living scattered, according to our tastes.

We bought this house and we share it. You will find my sisters as you walk about. As you can see, I live in the well.

'That's my last husband painted on the wall,' said the second princess, 'looking as though he were alive.'

She took me through her glass house showing me curiosities: the still-born foetus of the infamous Pope Joan who had so successfully posed as a Man of God until giving birth in the Easter parade. She had the tablets of stone on which Moses had received the Ten Commandments. The writing was blurred but it was easy to make out the gouged lines of the finger of God.

'I collect religious items.'

She had not minded her husband much more than any wife does until he had tried to stop her hobby.

'He built a bonfire and burned the body of a saint. The saint was very old and wrapped in cloth. I liked him about the house; he added something.'

After that she had wrapped her own husband in cloth and gone on wrapping the stale bandages round and round until she reached his nose. She had a moment's regret, and continued.

'He walked in beauty,' she said.

'His eyes were brown marshes, his lashes were like willow trees. His eyebrows shot together made a dam between his forehead and his face. His cheeks were steep and sheer, his mouth was a volcano. His breath was like a dragon's and his heart was torn from a bull. The sinews in his neck were white columns leading to the bolts of his collar-bone. I can still trace the cavity of his throat. His chest was a strongbox, his ribs were made of brass, they shone through his skin when the sun was out. His shoulder-blades were mountain ranges, his spine a cobbled road. His belly was filled with jewels and his cock woke at dawn. Fields of wheat still remind me of his hair, and when I see a hand whose fingers are longer than its palm I think it might be him come to touch me again.

'But he never touched me. It was a boy he loved. I pierced them with a single arrow where they lay.

'I still think it was poetic.'

My husband married me so that his liaisons with other women, being forbidden, would be more exciting. Danger was an aphrodisiac to him: he wanted nothing easy or gentle. His way was to cause whirlwinds. I was warned, we always are, by well-wishers or malcontents, but I chose to take no interest in gossip. My husband was handsome and clever. What did it matter if he needed a certain kind of outlet, so long as he loved me? I wanted to love him; I was determined to be happy with him. I had not been happy before.

At first I hardly minded his weeks away. I did not realize that part of his sport was to make me mad. Only then, when he had hurt me, could he fully enjoy the other beds he visited.

I soon discovered that the women he preferred were the inmates of a lunatic asylum. With them he arranged mock marriages in deserted barns. They wore a shroud as their wedding dress and carried a bunch of carrots as a bouquet. He had them straight after on a pig-trough altar. Most were virgins. He like to come home to me smelling of their blood.

Does the body hate itself so much that it seeks release at any cost?

I didn't kill him. I left him to walk the battlements of his ruined kingdom; his body was raddled with disease. The same winter he was found dead in the snow.

Why could he not turn his life towards me, as trees though troubled by the wind yet continue in the path of the sun?

You may have heard of Rapunzel.

Against the wishes of her family, who can best be described by their passion for collecting miniature dolls, she went to live in a tower with an older woman.

Her family were so incensed by her refusal to marry the prince next door that they vilified the couple, calling one a witch and the other a little girl. Not content with names, they ceaselessly tried to break into the tower, so much so that the happy pair had to seal up any entrance that was not on a level with the sky. The lover got in by climbing up Rapunzel's hair, and Rapunzel got in by nailing a wig to the floor and shinning up the tresses flung out of the window. Both of them could have used a ladder, but they were in love.

One day the prince, who had always liked to borrow his mother's frocks, dressed up as Rapunzel's lover and dragged himself into the tower. Once inside he tied her up and waited for the wicked witch to arrive. The moment she leaped through the window, bringing their dinner for the evening, the prince hit her over the head and threw her out again. Then he carried Rapunzel down the rope he had brought with him and forced her to watch while he blinded her broken lover in a field of thorns.

After that they lived happily ever after, of course.

As for me, my body healed, though my eyes never did, and eventually I was found by my sisters, who had come in their various ways to live on this estate.

My own husband?

Oh well, the first time I kissed him he turned into a frog. There he is, just by your foot. His name's Anton.

On New Year's Day, walking through the deep lanes slatted with light, I saw my husband on horseback, wearing his pink coat. He held his hunting horn to his lips and stood in the stirrups. The hunt rode off; soon they were only as big as holly berries hidden in the green.

I walked on, away from the path, through bushes and brambles, frightening partridges and threading a route between the patient cattle whose hooves in the mud were braceleted with beads of water. My boots were thick with mud. Every step was harder and harder to take. Soon I was lifting my feet as you would to climb a ladder. I was angry and sweating. I wanted to get home but I couldn't hurry. I had to get home to fetch the punch into the great hall and fire it with bright blue flames.

Coming with much difficulty to the top of a hill I looked across the widening valley and saw where the snow still patched the fields like sheets left out to dry. I love the thorn hedges and the trees bare overnight as though some child had stubbornly collected all the leaves, refusing to leave even one for a rival.

I saw my own house, its chimneys smoking, its windows orange.

Another year.

Then a stag and five deer came out of the wood and across the fields in front of my eyes. The fields were fenced and the stag jumped over, turning his head to bring the others. Just for a second he remained in the air, but in that second of flight I remembered my past, when I had been free to fly, long ago, before this gracious landing and a houseful of things.

He disappeared into the dark and I turned my back on the house. The last thing I heard was the sound of the hunt clattering into the courtyard.

I never wanted anyone but her. I wanted to run my finger from the cleft in her chin down the slope of her breasts and across the level plains of her stomach to where I knew she would be wet. I wanted to turn her over and ski the flats of my hands down the slope of her back. I wanted to pioneer the secret passage of her arse.

When she lay down I massaged her feet with mint oil and cut her toenails with silver scissors. I coiled her hair into living snakes and polished her teeth with my saliva.

I pierced her ears and filled them with diamonds. I dropped belladonna into her eyes.

When she was sick I wiped her fever with my own towels and when she cried I kept her tears in a Ming vase.

There was no separation between us. We rose in the morning and slept at night as twins do. We had four arms and four legs, and in the afternoons, when we read in the cool orchard, we did so sitting back to back.

I liked to feel the snake of her spine.

We kissed often, our mouths filling up with tongue and teeth and spit and blood when I bit her lower lip, and with my hands I held her against my hip bone.

We made love often, especially in the afternoons with t' blinds half pulled and the cold flag floor against our bodies.

For eighteen years we lived alone in a windy castle and saw no one but each other. Then someone found us and then it was too late.

The man I had married was a woman. They came to burn her. I killed her with a single blow to the head before they reached the gates, and fled that place, and am come here now.

I still have a coil of her hair.

We had been married a few years when a man came to the door selling brushes. My husband was at work so I let the man into our kitchen and gave him something to eat. I asked him to show me his bag and he spread out, as you would imagine, a layer of polishing clothes, a pile of round soaps, combs for the hair, combs for the beard of a billy goat, ordinary household things. I bought one or two useful pieces, then I asked him what he had in his other bag, the one he hadn't opened.

'What was it you wanted?' he asked.

'Poison . . .'

'Yes, for the rats.'

'No, for my husband.'

He seemed unsurprised by my intention to murder and opened the other bag. I looked inside. It was full of little jars and sealed bags.

'Is your husband a big man?'

'Very. He is very, very fat. He is the fattest man in the village. He has always been fat. He has eleven brothers, all of whom are as slender as spring corn. Every day he eats one cow followed by one pig.'

'You are right to kill him,' said the man. 'Put this in his milk at bedtime.'

Bedtime came and I stirred my husband's vat of milk and put in the powder as directed. My husband came crashing over to the stove and gulped the milk in one draught. As soon as he had finished he began to swell up. He swelled out of the house, cracking the roof, and within a few moments had exploded. Out of his belly came a herd of cattle and a fleet of pigs, all blinking in the light and covered in milk.

He had always complained about his digestion.

I rounded them up and set off to find my sisters. I prefer farming to cookery.

He called me Jess because that is the name of the hood which restrains the falcon.

I was his falcon. I hung on his arm and fed at his hand.

He said my nose was sharp and cruel and that my eyes had madness in them. He said I would tear him to pieces if he dealt softly with me.

At night, if he was away, he had me chained to our bed. It was a long chain, long enough for me to use the chamber pot or to stand at the window and wait for the late owls. I love to hear the owls. I love to see the sudden glide of wings spread out for prey, and then the dip and the noise like a lover in pain.

He used the chain when we went riding together. I had a horse as strong as his, and he'd whip the horse from behind and send it charging through the trees, and he'd follow, half a head behind, pulling on the chain and asking me how I liked my ride.

His game was to have me sit astride him when we made love and hold me tight in the small of my back. He said he had to have me above him, in case I picked his eyes out in the faltering candlelight.

I was none of these things, but I became them.

At night, in June I think, I flew off his wrist and tore his liver from his body, and bit my chain in pieces and left him on the bed with his eyes open.

He looked surprised, I don't know why. As your lover describes you, so you are.

When my husband had an affair with someone else I watched his eyes glaze over when we ate dinner together and I heard him singing to himself without me, and when he tended the garden it was not for me.

He was courteous and polite; he enjoyed being at home, but in the fantasy of his home I was not the one who sat opposite him and laughed at his jokes. He didn't want to change anything; he liked his life. The only thing he wanted to change was me.

It would have been better if he had hated me, or if he had abused me, or if he had packed his new suitcases and left.

As it was he continued to put his arm round me and talk about building a new wall to replace the rotten fence that divided our garden from his vegetable patch. I knew he would never leave our house. He had worked for it.

Day by day I felt myself disappearing. For my husband I was no longer a reality, I was one of the things around him. I was the fence which needed to be replaced. I watched myself in the mirror and saw that I was no longer vivid and exciting. I was worn and grey like an old sweater you can't throw out but won't put on.

He admitted he was in love with her, but he said he loved me.

Translated, that means, I want everything. Translated, that means, I don't want to hurt you yet. Translated, that means, I don't know what to do, give me time.

Why, why should I give you time? What time are you giving me? I am in a cell waiting to be called for execution.

I loved him and I was in love with him. I didn't use language to make a war-zone of my heart.

'You're so simple and good,' he said, brushing the hair from my face.

He meant, Your emotions are not complex like mine. My dilemma is poetic.

But there was no dilemma. He no longer wanted me, but he wanted our life.

Eventually, when he had been away with her for a few days and returned restless and conciliatory, I decided not to wait in my cell any longer. I went to where he was sleeping in another

57

room and I asked him to leave. Very patiently he asked me to remember that the house was his home, that he couldn't be expected to make himself homeless because he was in love.

'Medea did,' I said, 'and Romeo and Juliet, and Cressida, and Ruth in the Bible.'

He asked me to shut up. He wasn't a hero.

'Then why should I be a heroine?'

He didn't answer, he plucked at the blanket.

I considered my choices.

I could stay and be unhappy and humiliated.

I could leave and be unhappy and dignified.

I could beg him to touch me again.

I could live in hope and die of bitterness.

I took some things and left. It wasn't easy, it was my home too.

I hear he's replaced the back fence.

As soon as we were married my husband took me to his family home, far from anyone I knew. He promised me a companion and a library but asked me never to interrupt him during the day. I saw him at night for a few hours, over our dinner, though he never ate much. Nor did he seem anxious to decorate my bed with his body.

I asked him what he did during the day and he said he exercised his mind over the problems of Creation. I realized this could take some time and resigned myself to forgetting the rules of normal life.

One night, as we were eating a pigeon I had shot, my husband stood up and said, 'There is a black tower where wild beasts live. The tower has no windows and no doors. No one may enter or leave. At the top of the tower is a cage whose bars are made of bone. From this cage a trapped spirit peeps at the sun. The tower is my body, the cage is my skull, the spirit singing to comfort itself is me. But I am not comforted, I am alone. Kill me.'

I did as he asked. I smashed his skull with a silver candlestick and I heard a hissing noise like damp wood on the fire. I opened the doors and dragged his body into the air, and in the air he flew away.

I still see him sometimes, but only in the distance.

Their stories ended, the twelve dancing princesses invited me to spend the night as their guest.

'Someone is missing,' I said. 'There are only eleven of you and I have only heard eleven stories. Where is your sister?'

They looked at one another, then the eldest said, 'Our youngest sister is not here. She never came to live with us. On her wedding day to the prince who had discovered our secret, she flew from the altar like a bird from a snare and walked a tightrope between the steeple of the church and the mast of a ship weighing anchor in the bay.

'She was, of all of us, the best dancer, the one who made her body into shapes we could not follow. She did it for pleasure, but there was something more for her; she did it because any other life would have been a lie. She didn't burn in secret with a passion she could not express; she shone.

'We have not seen her for years and years, not since that day when we were dressed in red with our black hair unbraided. She must be old now, she must be stiff. Her body can only be a memory. The body she has will not be the body she had.'

'Do you remember,' said another sister, 'how light she was? She was so light that she could climb down a rope, cut it and tie it again in mid-air without plunging to her death. The winds supported her.'

'What was her name?'

'Fortunata.'

1649

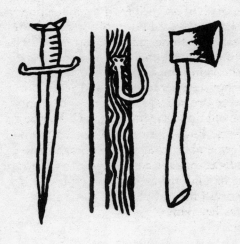

AT FIRST THE Civil War hardly touched us. Opinions were high, and there were those like Preacher Scroggs and Neighbour Firebrace who would have taken any opportunity to feel themselves above the common crowd. But it was a quiet enough affair, local battles and the Roundhead mob sometimes descending on a lordly house and claiming it for themselves in the name of God. There was no real feeling that the King would not win as he had always won, as kings have always won, whomever they fight.

I like a fight myself, and enjoyed baiting Neighbour Firebrace. Indeed I sorely missed his crooked face while I was in Wimbledon. With everyone in accord, what merriment is there?

At Wimbledon we were sure that at any moment Queen Henrietta would return with allies from France or Italy or Spain and sweep away the snivelling Puritans dressed in starch. But she found no allies. Well-wishers in plenty, but no allies. And the navy was against the King and controlling the ports and watching the seas for any sign of help.

When the King's men came to the house and told us stories of 'King Noll' as they parodied Cromwell, smashing the beautiful glass in our churches and closing up every place of distraction so that men and women might have nothing to occupy them but the invisible God, we grew to hate what had been only a joke.

I went to a church not far from the gardens. A country church famed for its altar window where our Lord stood feeding the five thousand. Black Tom Fairfax, with nothing better to do, had set up his cannon outside the window and given the order to fire. There was no window when I got there and the men had ridden away.

There was a group of women gathered round the remains of the glass which coloured the floor brighter than any carpet of flowers in a parterre. They were women who had cleaned the window, polishing the slippery fish our Lord had blessed in his outstretched hands, scraping away the candle smoke from the feet of the Apostles. They loved the window. Without speaking, and in common purpose, the women began to gather the pieces of the window in their baskets. They gathered the broken bread, and the two fishes, and the astonished faces of the hungry, until their baskets overflowed as the baskets of the disciples had overflowed in the original miracle. They gathered every piece, and they told me, with hands that bled, that they would rebuild the window in a secret place. At evening, their work done, they filed into the little church to pray, and I, not daring to follow, watched them through the hole where the window had been.

They kneeled in a line by the altar, and on the flag floor behind them, invisible to them, I saw the patchwork colours of the window, red and yellow and blue. The colours sank into the stone and covered the backs of the women, who looked as though they were wearing harlequin coats. The church danced in light. I left them there and walked home, my head full of things that cannot be destroyed.

The trial began on 20 January 1649. Jordan and Tradescant and I had been in London for a week. Tradescant put up at the Crown of Thorns and Jordan and I went back to our old home, not visited for six years.

The smells were the same, the river was still filthy, the dredgers still bobbed about up to their necks in rubbish. In the middle of the river was a chicken on a crate. I felt proud and excited, wanting even to bump into my scrawny witch of a counterfeit friend, if only to tell her of our success in the world.

Jordan was nineteen and stood as tall as my chest, which was impressive for a man not come out of my body. He resembled me not at all, a thing which must have been a secret relief to him, though he never shuddered in my company as others do.

I was wearing my best dress, the one with a wide skirt that

would serve as a sail for some war-torn ship, and a bit of fancy lace at the neck, made by a blind woman who had intended it to be a shawl. I had given her some estimate of my dimensions, but she would not believe me and so, although I have nothing to go round my shoulders save a dozen blankets sewn together, I do have a fine-worked collar. I had got out my hat for the occasion of our homecoming, and despite my handicaps I cut something of a fine figure, I thought.

As we neared our long hut I saw smoke coming from the hole in the roof and, getting closer, spotted Neighbour Firebrace and Preacher Scroggs standing together on my front step, deep in viperous chatter.

'Jordan,' I cried. 'Run as fast as you can, they are burning us away.'

I ran up to them and towered above them as Goliath over David, and they trembled, and Preacher Scroggs mumbled something behind his hand about my being dead.

'Who told you I was dead?'

Scroggs had no answer to that, and I pushed him aside as you would a ninepin and looked in the hut.

It was stacked to the roof with broadsheets.

'We have requisitioned your house for Jesus and Oliver Cromwell,' said Firebrace, his cranesbill nose red with righteousness. 'These are papers denouncing the King.'

I snatched one from the top of the pile and found it to be a copy of 'A Perfect Diurnal', a foul and hackish screed written by Samuel Peck, a man well known for his knavery and misdeeds.

'This Peck,' I said, seizing Firebrace by his jacket, 'this Peck is an enemy of mine, having taken two good dogs and never paid for them, and that some years back.'

Firebrace started his wriggling, so I lifted him clean from the floor and brought him to my eye level. He began to dribble.

'This Peck,' I continued, my breath as fiery as a dragon, 'is a bald-headed buzzard. A tall, thin-faced fellow with a hawk's nose, a meagre countenance and long runagate legs. Constant in nothing but wenching, lying and drinking.'

I called to Jordan to start throwing out the newspapers.

'Make a pile, Jordan, make it as high as you like and we'll have a full blaze and happen put Preacher Scroggs and Neighbour Firebrace on the top in memory of Guy Fawkes.'

Then Scroggs came up to me, his eyes oozing venom, his face as contorted as a spitfrog.

'You are in danger of Hell, madam.'

'Then pity me,' says I. 'I pity you, for you are in no danger, it being quite certain that you entered Hell a time ago and will not be returning.'

'Perhaps you should tell that to my men,' he says, and standing back with his twisted smile revealed eight sober Roundheads in their coats of no colours.

I went to the door and saw another three surrounding Jordan as he made the bonfire.

'Satan's league!' I shouted. 'Get thee behind me!'

Because I am a sinner the devils did not vanish as they did for Jesus; rather they took hold of Jordan and began to march him away while Firebrace set up such a farting and laughing that I feared he would explode before I had time to dismember him.

I ran straight at the guards, broke the arms of the first, ruptured the second and gave the third a kick in the head that knocked him out at once. The other five came at me, and when I had dispatched two for an early judgement another took his musket and fired me straight in the chest. I fell over, killing the man who was poised behind me, and plucked the musket ball out of my cleavage. I was in a rage then.

'You are no gentleman to spoil a poor woman's dress, and my best dress at that.'

I sat up and rolled up my sleeves, for it dawned on me that I must take these scurvy fellows seriously. But before I had managed my feet they had run away, leaving only Scroggs and Firebrace trembling the way they will on the Last Day.

'I will not kill you now,' I said, 'for I am tired after my journey and wish only to settle in my own house. Slink away with droppings in your pants and never come here again, not even if I go away for a lifetime.'

At my magnanimousness they were abashed, as even sinners must be in the presence of virtue. When they had gone

Jordan and I piled up all the copies of 'A Perfect Diurnal' and made a bonfire whose light blazed across the Thames in streaks of splendour. The very poor came and sat by it, and warmed themselves, and drank beer of mine. I fancied I had never been away and that all our adventures and troubles were a dream. I looked at Jordan and saw a little boy with a battered boat. And I thought, if only the fire could be kept burning, the future might be kept at bay and this moment would remain. This warmth, this light. But I fell asleep and woke shivering to see the early morning hanging over the water and the chars of our fire petrified with frost.

I was drinking with Tradescant when a boy slipped into the Crown of Thorns and put a broadsheet on our table.

The innkeeper was a Loyalist and had no truck with those po-faced, flat-buttocked zealots who had declared the King a traitor to his own people. A despot, they called him, a tyrant, a spendthrift, unwilling to accept a Parliament of the people for the people. London was awash with pamphlets telling anyone who could read them that the King had no Divine Right and should be called to justice for his sins. For myself, I would rather live with sins of excess than sins of denial.

The Puritans, who wanted a rule of saints on earth, and no king but Jesus, forgot that we are born into flesh and in flesh must remain. Their women bind their breasts and cook plain food without salt, and the men are so afraid of their member uprising that they keep it strapped between their legs with bandages.

This week, the week before the trial, they are paying men to sit in public houses and overhear any loyalty to the King. This badly printed broadsheet with a message from the King and no publisher's name was a crime punishable by death for those who put it about. The boy had gone, seeped into the wainscot with a penny from Tradescant, and all of us who love the King crowded round to hear his words.

67

Tradescant had promised us seats in the gallery at the trial. We are going in disguise, though what disguise I shall assume is not yet clear . . .

There was an order in London during the week of the trial prohibiting the presence of Cavaliers, and Tradescant was in serious danger, being a chosen employee of the Royal house. Everyone anxious to attend the trial was subjected to a rigorous search and investigation, though the Puritans, concerned to uphold their public image, had promised an open trial, free to all, except supporters of the King. Tradescant and Jordan dressed themselves as drabs, with painted faces and scarlet lips and dresses that looked as though they'd been pawed over by every infantryman in the capital. Jordan had a fine mincing walk and a leer that got him a good few offers of a bed for the night.

I swathed myself about in rags, black as pitch, and put on an old wig we begged from a theatrical. Then I made myself a specially reinforced wheelbarrow and sat in it like a heap of manure.

In this way we made our entrance to the Cotton House and the trial of the King.

Two soldiers stopped us and asked if we had been given passes to the gallery.

'Oh, sir, passes we have,' I sighed, reaching into my filthy folds. 'We have been granted passes on account of our sinfulness. Look, they are marked by Hugh Peter himself.'

It was true. Hugh Peter, a puce-stained pock-marked preacher who thought himself Chirst's deputy, had offered passes to the gallery for any sinners who truly longed to repent and see the Rule of Saints begin. He had preached his sermon that week on the text, 'He shall bind their King in chains', and afterwards the hopeless and the damned had crept to him for solace. Jordan, in his costume as a drab, had felt Hugh Peter's oily hand slide under his skirts promising the freedom that only Christ can bring. Jordan had wept and moaned and begged two more passes for other friends of his. Common women, women in need of a pastor's touch.

And here we were.

The soldier squinted at the bits of paper and asked me to leave my wheelbarrow at the entrance to the gallery.

'I cannot, sir,' I cried, 'for I have the Clap and my flesh is rotting beneath me. If I were to stand up, sir, you would see a river of pus run across these flags. The Rule of Saints cannot begin in pus.'

Jordan and Tradescant stood behind me, each holding a handle of the wheelbarrow.

'My daughter and my niece, sir,' I said, waving a hand. 'These two have pushed me from Plymouth so that I can be redeemed.'

'We have,' said Jordan, 'every mile a torment.'

The soldiers turned aside and conferred amongst themselves, while I sweated for fear they would make me stand up and thus see my size. Since my battle with the guards Tradescant had told me there was a warrant for my arrest.

'You may go in,' said one of the soldiers.

'Then, please,' said I, rolling my eyes winningly, 'please, clear a path for us, for I will have to stagger up the steps into the gallery while my daughter catches any fluids that may flow from me. It is the stench of a three days' dead dog and not for the noses of the tender.'

I saw the soldier's lips twitch, but he said nothing and led us to the great doors leading up to the gallery. He pushed aside the queue waiting for admittance and waved us through.

Once the doors had thudded behind us I leapt from the barrow, picked it up and ran to the top of the stairs where I immediately jumped back in and recommenced my groaning and calling out to Jesus.

The trial lasted seven days, and it was no trial but a means to an execution. The King in his velvet hat, with no jewels about him but his Star of the Garter, bore up proudly in the face of Bradshaw, the chief prosecutor. He won sympathy even from his enemies. On Sunday, when religious folk were at church, Obadiah Sedgewick denounced the King as usual from his pulpit in Covent Garden, and met with silence.

On the seventh day the gallery was packed with goggle-eyed ruffians all in their Puritan clothes come to hear sentence. The clerk stood up and read through all the King's misdeeds, including that of refusing to plead guilty or not guilty because he would not recognize the authority of the court. At length this stick of a man with a spotted youth's face and the balding skull of an ancient read out, solemn as he could, 'Charles Stuart, Tyrant, Traitor, Murderer and Public Enemy, you shall be put to death by the severing of your head from your body.'

Then all the commissioners who had signed the death warrant, sixty-eight of them, stood up to signify their agreement.

The King tried to speak, but Bradshaw would have none of it and motioned for him to be led away. The King was already dead in law, and a dead man cannot speak.

We watched the King leave the chamber, his back straight, his cane in his hand. At the doorway to the street he saw crowds of his followers, flouting the ban on their presence, too many for the guards to arrest but still unable to reach the courtroom. They were weeping. Charles turned to his gaolers and said, in a voice loud enough for all of us to hear, 'You may forbid their attendance, but not their tears.'

In winter the frost at midnight brightens the ground and hardens the stars. We kept vigil all night, the three of us, huddled together, watching the execution platform being built by the light of a dozen flares. The carpenters wore black masks and kept looking about them as though they expected a troop of demons to ride through the darkness and claim them. It is bad luck to kill a king.

The executioner himself stood underneath a torch in the wall, sharpening his axe with a whetstone. He sharpened, and the sparks flew in orange spikes. He tested the blade with his thumb, and we saw it run red. There was a sheep in a cage near-by. It was the custom to try out the axe beforehand for those of noble birth. Two men took the sheep struggling from the cage and held it, its legs buckled underneath itself, while the executioner with a single straight swing whistled through the fleece and the muscle and the bone and did it so clean that I fancied I might pick up the head and sew it back on and let the sheep run off.

There was a half-hearted cheer from the crew, who ran a skewer through the animal's body and put it to roast over their fires. The head and the fleece were given to a beggar.

It was not until the afternoon that the King appeared in his linen shirt, his beard trimmed and nothing of him shivering, though many a spectator had fainted with cold. He knelt down and rested his head on the block, and I saw Tradescant's face stream with tears that froze at once and lay on his cheeks like diamonds. The King gave the signal, and a moment later his head was wrapped in a white cloth and his body was carried away.

In the Crown of Thorns that night Tradescant made plans to take ship and leave us. I saw the look on Jordan's face and my heart became a captive in a locked room. I couldn't reach him now. I knew he would go.

I went outside and walked until the lights of the inn were specks in the distance and I was alone with the river flowing out to sea.

At a dancing school in a remote place, Fortunata teaches her pupils to become points of light.

They begin with her as early as six or seven and some stay for the rest of their lives.

Most, she releases like butterflies over a flowering world. Bodies that could have bent double and grown numb she maintains as metal in a fiery furnace, tempering, stretching, forcing sinews into impossible shapes and calling her art nature.

She believes that we are fallen creatures who once knew how to fly. She says that light burns in our bodies and threatens to dissolve us at any moment. How else can we account for so many of us who disappear?

It is her job to channel the light lying in the solar plexus, along the arms, along the legs, forcing it into fingertips and feet, forcing it out so that her dancers sweat tongues of flame.

To her dancers she says, 'Through the body, the body is conquered.'

She asks them to meditate on a five-pointed star in the belly and to watch the points push outwards, the fifth point into the head. She spins them, impaled with light, arms upraised, one leg at a triangle across the other thigh, one foot, on point, on a penny coin, and spins them, until all features are blurred, until the human being most resembles a freed spirit from a darkened jar. One after the other she spins them, like a juggler keeping plates on sticks; one after the other she runs up and down the line as one slows or another threatens to fall from dizziness. And at a single moment, when all are spinning in harmony down the long hall, she hears music escaping from their heads and backs and livers and spleens. Each has a tone like cut glass. The noise is deafening. And it is then that the spinning seems to stop, that the wild gyration of the dancers passes from movement into infinity.

Who are they that shine in gold like Apostles in a church window at midday?

The polished wooden floor glows with the heat of their bodies, and one by one they crumble over and lie exhausted on the ground.

Fortunata refreshes them and the dance begins again.

In the world there is a horror of plagues. Of mysterious diseases that wipe out towns and cities, leaving empty churches and bedclothes that must be burned. Holy water and crosses and mountain air and the protection of saints and a diet of watercress are all thought to save us as a species from rotting. But what can save us as a species from love? A man sold me a necklace made of chicken bones; he said these chickens were the direct descendants of the chickens who had scratted around the crib at Bethlehem. The bones would save me from pain of every kind and lead me piously to Heaven. He was wearing some himself.

'And love?' I said. 'And love?'

He shook his head and assured me that nothing was proof against love. Not even the slightest amourette could be forestalled by an amulet. Bringing it on, though, was another matter – did I want a bag of spices mixed by Don Juan himself?

'But surely if it can be encouraged it can also be prevented?'

'Not at all,' said the man, 'for everyone is inclined to love. It is easy to bring on, impossible to end until it ends itself.'

'And yet some people never love. My mother is one such.'

He said, 'They have a secret somewhere. Usually.'

I thought of the great lovers, men and women who had made it their profession, who had tirelessly leapt from one passion to another, sometimes running two, three or four at once like a stunt charioteer. What were they looking for?

My own passions had nothing to recommend them. Not only was I chasing a dancer who, on the evidence of her sisters, was too old to move, I had in the past entangled myself

73

in numerous affairs with women who would not, could not or did not love me. And did I love them? I thought so at the time, though now I have come to doubt it, seeing only that I loved myself through them.

On more than one occasion I have been ready to abandon my whole life for love. To alter everything that makes sense to me and to move into a different world where the only known will be the beloved. Such a sacrifice must be the result of love . . . or is it that the life itself was already worn out? I had finished with that life, perhaps, and could not admit it, being stubborn or afraid, or perhaps did not know it, habit being a great binder.

I think it is often so that those most in need of change choose to fall in love and then throw up their hands and blame it all on fate. But it is not fate, at least, not if fate is something outside of us; it is a choice made in secret after nights of longing.

When I have shaken off my passion, somewhat as a dog shakes off an unexpected plunge into the canal, I find myself without any understanding of what it was that ravaged me. The beloved is shallow, witless, heartless, mercenary, calculating, silly. Naturally these thoughts protect me, but they also render me entirely gullible or without discrimination.

And so I will explain it as follows.

A man or woman sunk in dreams that cannot be spoken, about a life they do not possess, comes suddenly to a door in the wall. They open it. Beyond the door is that life and a man or a woman to whom it is already natural. It may not be possessions they want, it may very well be the lack of them, but the secret life is suddenly revealed. This is their true home and this is their beloved.

I may be cynical when I say that very rarely is the beloved more than a shaping spirit for the lover's dreams. And perhaps such a thing is enough. To be a muse may be enough. The pain is when the dreams change, as they do, as they must. Suddenly the enchanted city fades and you are left alone again in the windy desert. As for your beloved, she didn't understand you. The truth is, you never understood yourself.

In one city I visited, the entire population had been wiped out by love three times in a row. After the third occasion the only two survivors, a monk and a whore, determined that love should be illegal in their new state and that anyone found indulging in it would be put to death. Cheered by their admirable plan the two of them made love as often as possible and, thanks to the sturdiness of the whore, were soon able to re-fill the city with inhabitants. From their earliest moment children were warned of the dire consequences, personal and social, of love. They were urged to put aside any romantic fancies, the sexes were carefully segregated and all marriages were arranged. Sex itself, tending as it does to fire the heart as well as the groin, was possible only for the purposes of childbearing, or on the three festival nights when a troop of male and female prostitutes were hired from a neighbouring town and asked to satisfy the longings of the city dwellers. Naturally, even after such brief encounters, there were those who vanished in the night. The monk and the whore, now fabulously old but still absolutely in control, declared all such vanishings illegal and sequestered the person's property.

I questioned them about their strictness, likening them to the Puritans holding sway in my own country. They had not heard of Puritanism, but found the idea of bandaging up the male member so as to leave it immovable very appealing. The religious side, they said, was unimportant; the urgency was to prevent another plague of love sweeping the city and causing its hardworking people to give up their jobs and families and take to flinging roses through the windows and composing ballads.

'A few months of that sort of thing,' said the monk, 'and the people are ruined.'

Then he told me how it had been the last time the plague had struck. It had started quietly enough, a few guitars in the moonlight, a few love-notes sent under cover of darkness. Then the mayor had fallen for a shop-girl and draped his chain of office over a public toilet. Then every single monk in the monastery was caught masturbating in front of a statue of Hildegard of Bingen. They ignored the call to prayer at five a.m. Indeed they ignored it for so long that the old man hired to ring the bell died of heart failure. He was still pulling at eight o'clock, and so were the monks.

Worse, ordinary men and women, with no eccentricity in their natures, began to eye one another and die for love. Every day new graves were dug in the hillside. The grave-digger himself was so struck by the woman he was burying that he wrenched the lid from her coffin and got in. After hours of pleading his family lost patience and threw the soil in themselves. After that the dead were thrown into the river, and then of course everyone who was left died of contamination. Except the monk, who was on a fast and drinking only holy water from the monastery cellar, and the whore, who drank no water at all.

'The people who live here now,' he said, 'are completely happy and disease-free. You should settle here yourself. It would do you good.'

I decided to look round the place and began by going to a stall to buy some bread. The young woman behind the stall was unsmiling, though I smiled a good deal. Eventually she said, 'What you're doing is illegal. You should stop it.'

'What's illegal?'

'Falling in love with me.'

'I'm not falling in love with you.'

'Why are you smiling then?'

Before I could answer she pulled out a book and looked under 'S' in the index. She read out loud: 'Smiling is one of the earliest signs of love. If someone smiles at you, be sure they have another intention.'

'I'm very sorry,' I said, my teeth in a straight line.

After that I went to buy a mouth-organ, and I was very careful not to smile at all.

'Have you a little guitar or a mandolin?' I asked.

I might as well have asked for the bones of the Holy Mother to be dug up, so wrathful and insulted did the shop-keeper appear. I explained I was a stranger, and he softened a little and told me that guitars and mandolins were forbidden, as were violins. He had a nice tuba, if I was interested. Politely,

I declined the tuba and waited for some enlightenment. He directed me to the city museum.

The museum was a gloomy edifice. No one seemed to be looking after it; there were no guides and no other visitors. It was a Museum of Love. As I walked into the main chamber I was greeted by a statue of Samson, blind and defeated, chained between two pillars in the fleshy palace of the Philistines. Sitting at his heel, laughing gleefully, was Delilah. She was holding his hair.

Very soon I found the outlawed guitars and mandolins. They were hung high on the wall, and underneath was a fierce inscription describing them as: 'INSTRUMENTS OF LUST AND FURY'.

Near-by was a bunch of dried red roses. Over there, Cupid's bow and arrow. There were stale sugar hearts in glass cases, and bad poems pinned firmly to the table. Saddest of all was a carefully stuffed small dog with a bow round its neck. The medallion said: 'I LOVE YOU'.

I was very sorry to see under the section marked 'PROFLIGATES AND WANTONS AND THE HARM THEY HAVE CAUSED' our own King Henry towering over his unfortunate wives.

Since I was alone, with no one to challenge me, I reached up and took the guitar from the wall. I blew away the dust and tested the strings. They were loose but not rotten. I carefully tuned them one by one and strummed a gentle chord.

I had been singing quietly for a while when I noticed a pair of feet in front of me. Then another pair and another. I was surrounded by the citizens. They said nothing to me and, seeing there was no escape, I continued to play. Gradually, singing as if in a trance, they began to join in, and one or two slipped their arms around the waists of their companions. We continued in this way until it was almost dark; then one of the men, an innkeeper, shouted that we must all join him in a celebration and that I must come too, and continue my tunes. We straggled out into the night, and at the inn one of the women set up Cupid's bow and arrow over the bar. She laughed – she didn't know what it was, but it was forbidden and she liked it. About midnight, as I was thinking of going to sleep, a shouting and wailing began in the street outside.

It was the monk on his purple pallet and the whore on her burnished throne. They had come with the Chief of Police. I wasted no time, but fled through the window holding on to the guitar. The girl slung the bow and arrow over my body and blew me a kiss.

Much later, years later, I heard that from that night the plague of love had overtaken the city once more, but this time it had not followed the normal pattern. The monk had gathered together the entire citizenry and warned them that unless they gave up their wicked ways at once they would all die. The penalty for love, he reminded them, was death. They took a vote and unanimously agreed to be put to death. The monk and the whore shot them all and found themselves alone. They would have to begin again. Wearily they climbed into bed.

When I left the city where love is an epidemic I rejoined Tradescant's ship and we continued our course towards the Bermudas. It was Tradescant's plan to stock up with seeds and pods and any exotic thing that might take the fancy of the English and so be natural in our gardens. It was our hope to make more of a success of the new fashion of grafting, which we had understood from France, and had already been done to some satisfaction on certain fruit trees.

Grafting is the means whereby a plant, perhaps tender or uncertain, is fused into a hardier member of its strain, and so the two take advantage of each other and produce a third kind, without seed or parent. In this way fruits have been made resistant to disease and certain plants have learned to grow where previously they could not.

There are many in the Church who condemn this practice as unnatural, holding that the Lord who made the world made its flora as he wished and in no other way.

Tradescant has been praised in England for his work with the cherry, and it was on the cherry that I first learned the art of grafting and wondered whether it was an art I might apply to myself.

My mother, when she saw me patiently trying to make a

yield between a Polstead Black and a Morello, cried two things: 'Thou mayest as well try to make a union between thyself and me by sewing us at the hip,' and then, 'Of what sex is that monster you are making?'

I tried to explain to her that the tree would still be female although it had not been born from seed, but she said such things had no gender and were a confusion to themselves.

'Let the world mate of its own accord,' she said, 'or not at all.'

But the cherry grew, and we have sexed it and it is female.

What I would like is to have some of Tradescant grafted on to me so that I could be a hero like him. He will flourish in any climate, pack his ships with precious things and be welcomed with full honours when the King is restored.

England is a land of heroes, every boy knows that.

I slipped away from our main ship soon after we had weighed anchor, to fetch water and make a tour of the islands. Tradescant never objected to these wanderings: he took it for granted that I would bring something back to justify my absence. And he knew I liked to be alone, a habit I have learned from my mother, who has always been alone.

As I rowed towards an inhospitable-looking rock it became clear to me that when I think about her, or dream about her, she is always huge and I am always tiny. I'm sitting on her hand, the way she holds her puppies, and picking at her face for something, I don't know what. She's laughing, and so am I.

She is like a mathematical equation, always there and impossible to disprove.

I think she may have been found herself, long before she found me. I imagine her on the bank, in a bottle. The bottle is cobalt blue with a wax stopper wrapped over a piece of rag. A woman coming by hears noises from the bottle, and taking her knife she cuts open the seal and my mother comes thickening out like a genie from a jar, growing bigger and bigger and finally solidifying into her own proportions. She grants the woman three wishes and throws the bottle out to sea, and now she has forgotten all that and sits with her dogs watching the tide.

Above me the gulls burst in white battalions, and ahead of me the tall rocks loom. To the north of this tiny island is a tract of sand where the sea cuts through like a tongue. I will pull up my boat at this deep divided shore and see what signs of life there are. Islands are metaphors for the heart, no matter what poet says otherwise.

My own heart, like this wild place, has never been visited, and I do not know whether it could sustain life.

In an effort to find out I am searching for a dancer who may or may not exist, though I was never conscious of beginning this journey. Only in the course of it have I realized its true aim. When I left England I thought I was running away. Running away from uncertainty and confusion but most of all running away from myself. I thought I might become someone else in time, grafted on to something better and stronger. And then I saw that the running away was a running towards. An effort to catch up with my fleet-footed self, living another life in a different way.

I gave chase in a ship, but others make the journey without moving at all. Whenever someone's eyes glaze over, you have lost them. They are as far from you as if their body were carried at the speed of light beyond the compass of the world.

Time has no meaning, space and place have no meaning, on this journey. All times can be inhabited, all places visited. In a single day the mind can make a millpond of the oceans. Some people who have never crossed the land they were born on have travelled all over the world. The journey is not linear, it is always back and forth, denying the calendar, the wrinkles and lines of the body. The self is not contained in any moment or any place, but it is only in the intersection of moment and place that the self might, for a moment, be seen vanishing through a door, which disappears at once.

The earth is round and flat at the same time. This is obvious. That it is round appears indisputable; that it is flat is our common experience, also indisputable. The globe does not supersede the map; the map does not distort the globe.

Maps are magic. In the bottom corner are whales; at the top, cormorants carrying pop-eyed fish. In between is a subjective account of the lie of the land. Rough shapes of countries that may or may not exist, broken red lines marking paths that are at best hazardous, at worst already gone. Maps are constantly being re-made as knowledge appears to increase. But is knowledge increasing or is detail accumulating?

A map can tell me how to find a place I have not seen but have often imagined. When I get there, following the map faithfully, the place is not the place of my imagination. Maps, growing ever more real, are much less true.

And now, swarming over the earth with our tiny insect bodies and putting up flags and building houses, it seems that all the journeys are done.

Not so. Fold up the maps and put away the globe. If someone else had charted it, let them. Start another drawing with whales at the bottom and cormorants at the top, and in between identify, if you can, the places you have not found yet on those other maps, the connections obvious only to you. Round and flat, only a very little has been discovered.

HALLUCINATIONS AND DISEASES OF THE MIND

Objects 1 : A woman looks into her bag and recognizes none of her belongings. She hurries home. But where is home? She follows the address written in her purse. She has never seen this house before and who are those ugly children wrecking the garden? Inside a fat man is waiting for his supper. She shoots him. At the trial she says she had never seen him before. He was her husband.

Objects 2 : A man visits a famous country house. He strays from the guided tour and finds himself in a quiet sitting room he knows to be his own. He finds his pipe and book on the footstool where he left them. He reaches into the walnut cabinet for a glass of port. He remembers how happy he used to be in this place and doesn't understand at all why he later appears in court and has to pay a large fine for making free with a National Interest. What puzzles him most is where his dogs were. Usually the beagles are by the fire.

Time 1 : A young man on board an Admiralty salvage tug close to the mouth of the Thames goes on deck to look at the stars. His mates are asleep, the lifeboats firmly battened. A man stands next to him and says, 'I have heard they are burying the King at Windsor. It is more than a hundred years since Henry was left to rot there beneath a purple pall. Jane Seymour is beside him. No monarch has ever been buried there since. There is room for Charles, a little room.'

The young man turns astonished; he knows of no King, only a Queen, who is far from being dead. He opens his mouth to protest the joke and finds he is face to face with John Tradescant. Above them the sails whip in the wind.

Time 2 : They are cat-calling the girl as she comes out of school. She hates them, she wants to kill them. They tell her she smells, that she's too fat, too tall. She walks home along the river bank to a council flat in Upper Thames Street. The traffic deafens her. She climbs up the steps at Waterloo Bridge to look at St Paul's glinting in the evening. She can't see St Paul's. All she can see are rows of wooden stakes and uncertain craft bobbing along the water. She can't hear the traffic any more, the roar of dogs is deafening. Coming to herself, she kicks the bunch of hounds and drags her blanket shawl closer to her. For a moment she felt dizzy, lost her balance, but no, she's home as always. She can see her hut. She laughs, and the wind blows through the gaps in her teeth. Jordan will be waiting for her. She doesn't have to see him to know he's there.

Lies 1 : There is only the present and nothing to remember.

Lies 2 : Time is a straight line.

Lies 3 : The difference between the past and the future is that one has happened while the other has not.

Lies 4 : We can only be in one place at a time.

Lies 5 : Any proposition that contains the word 'finite' (the world, the universe, experience, ourselves . . .)

Lies 6 : Reality as something which can be agreed upon.

Lies 7 : Reality as truth.

Safe, sound and protected. That's how I wanted Jordan to be. When he left me I was proud and broken-hearted, but he came from the water and I knew the water would claim him again.

I carried on my old ways for a while, breeding the dogs and traipsing down to Hyde Park to show them off in a fight. The Puritans wanted an end to that too; they had in mind that a park should be a place to walk about, not a place to have an adventure and make a living. I have a mind to think that people can walk about anywhere, it's the other distractions they crave, even more so now that the death of the King has put an end to the future as a place we already know. Now the future is wild and waits for us as a beast in a lair.

I resolved for Jordan's sake, and Tradescant's, and the memory of the King, to spit on the Puritans whenever I passed them and to wear in my hair bright braids of clashing colour whenever I had occasion to be near one of their churches.

Many of them have set upon me for my insolence, and most of those are dead. Out of charity, such as I am famed for, I left one or two to be crippled.

One night as I was leaving Hyde Park, sawdust covering me as though I were a cow hung for meat, a man stepped out of the shadows and called me 'madam'. I have always been at the mercy of good manners, and so I listened politely, my head on one side, and agreed to go with him to a meeting house. He said it concerned the liberty of us all.

The meeting house, in a filthy inn off Blackfriar's fields, was already full when I arrived with my dogs. I had a barrel of water off them to revive the most bruised and bleeding, and then I sat quiet while a man in the cloth of Jesus led us in prayer and then asked us to consider two passages of the Old Testament.

He said 'Thou shalt not kill' is a tenet of our faith, but we should too be aware of another part of the Law of Moses: 'an eye for an eye and a tooth for a tooth'.

I have long been interested in these contradictions and looked forward to a full rendering of their meaning. The preacher went on to say that for us, as Royalists, avenging the King's murder was a matter of urgency, and yet we could not break the Holy Law.

I blushed here, having broken it many times.

'Then you must go in secret and quiet, and gouge out your enemies' eyes when you see them, and deprive them of their teeth if they have them. This fulfils the Law of God.'

I was very much taken with this rendering, and could only wonder how it had not come to me voluntarily before now. It is a thing to have learning and so be able to interpret the Scriptures.

We agreed to meet at the full and new moons to encourage one another, as the disciples of old.

I had only a little way to walk home, and hardly expected to find such an early opportunity to exercise my calling. Hearing a horse behind me I moved to one side, but not soon enough to escape the touch of a whip. I turned in a fury and saw it to be a pock-marked, leather-faced, drab-witted ancient, got up in grey with a flat lace collar too big for modesty. I pulled him

84

from his horse and popped his eyeballs with my thumbs, and then, forcing open his jaw as I would to get a chicken bone out of a dog, I loosened his teeth with my heel and soon had them mostly out and wrapped up in his own handkerchief.

By the time of the full moon I had done gallantly, I thought, and went to the meeting to hear stories of injury and revenge. I was suspicious to see that no one had brought any trophy of their right-doings, and so, as an encouragement, I tipped my sack of takings over the floor. I had 119 eyeballs, one missing on account of a man who had lost one already, and over 2,000 teeth.

A number of those in the room fainted immediately, and the preacher asked me to be less zealous in the next fortnight or, if I could not be, at least to leave my sack at home.

I was hurt by this; he had put no quota on our heads, and it seemed to me that my zeal had only made up for the sloth of others.

I did not stay for refreshments. I set off alone, and fed the eyeballs to my dogs and used the teeth as drainage for my watercress bed. I had decided to continue my sabotage alone when I was approached again by the whore from Spitalfields whom I hadn't seen for seven years. She was older and less beautiful but her figure showed the discipline of her trade. She seemed nervous and I wondered what it was she wanted from me.

It came to pass that she and her sisters, as she called them, had taken to murdering those Puritans who visited their brothel. Over this they had no difficulty – what troubled them was the disposal of the bodies. They would not trust a man to help, and already the bodies were so thick in the cellar that she feared an outbreak of the plague. Would I help? I was strong enough.

I had been lonely enough since Jordan had left, finding little in the way of companionship. Men and women seem sly-mouthed to me, and when they rub up against you purring friendship it is often a different thing they have in mind, something to their own advantage. I have been hurt before with my ready heart and I am wary now of blandishments and easy tongues.

I made up my mind to help her because of her straightforwardness and because bodies mean nothing to me, dead or alive. I would cry for my dogs and my boy but the rest may vanish as they please.

The brothel was a place of great skilfulness. When we came to the door a wooden flap was lifted and a pair of ferret eyes took us in. Inside there were noises of pain and misery such as we will hear in Hell. This counterfeit of the damned seemed strange to me, the more so when I was allowed to peep into a chamber and saw a man, naked but for a mask he wore, being branded on the buttocks with a hot iron. The woman who plunged the livid stick into his flesh was no taller than a child and looked a child from behind, though I was told she was well over sixty. When she turned around I saw her face was wrinkled and patched and her lips were white.

'Pig fat,' said my accomplice. 'She is entirely covered in pig fat but the lips are larded to whiten them.'

I asked why this was.

'The man is a farmer of pigs. He loves pigs, but his wife no longer allows him to creep into their hindparts with his member. He comes to us and we punish him for his temptations. Look.'

I put my eyes back to the flap and saw that the man had been branded with the sign of a rutting pig. He was groaning with pain, but when the dwarf woman turned him over with her still-hot prong his member was swollen and hard out in front of him with lust. I heard a snorting, and a pig was driven into the room, wild with fright. The man leaped at it and, holding it fast between his legs, continued his pleasure with deep thrusts while the dwarf heated up the iron again.

'Is this the usual manner of satisfaction?' I asked.

'There is no usual manner,' she said. 'There is only the unusual. These men are of God's Elect, do you not know? Surely God's Elect are entitled to pleasure?' Then she laughed hideously and told me the man was a great supporter of Cromwell and would be dead by morning.

'Do you trade only in Puritans then?'

'We trade in those who need us. Have you not seen their sheets with holes?'

I said I had not, but had heard of them from the wife of my parson, Preacher Scroggs.

'We have no shortage of preachers here,' she said. 'Look.'

She led to another door and opened the flap. On a low bed a woman was being entered in the usual position, but on top of the man was another man, clinging as a beetle to a raft and busy by the back passage.

'How heavy that must be for the woman,' I cried, and at the same moment the two men sat up and began embracing each other and wiping each other's faces with their emissions.

It was then that I recognized them.

'It is Preacher Scroggs and Neighbour Firebrace.'

My friend clapped her hand over my mouth and drew me into a private room where cakes were set out for the two of us. I explained my association with those unrepentant vermin and asked if I might have a favour in return for my pains with the bodies.

She said I might, and the next time Preacher Scroggs and Neighbour Firebrace visited the Spitalfields brothel this is what happened . . .

It was a fine night, the moon fair in the clouds, the weather warm. I had spent the few days previous constructing a revolving panel set in the wall. I fastened myself to the off side and waited for my clients to arrive.

Scroggs came in first, in a purple nightdress affair. Then Firebrace in a toga of some kind. They were to play Caesar and Brutus before the quarrel. Unable to contain myself, I waited long enough to see Firebrace's monstrous member rise beneath his skirts, then I swung into the wall and shot the revolving panel into the room. Both men screeched and were much taken aback, but they could not tell it was me, only some giant in the uniform of an executioner. My platform was an executioner's dais and I had a block upon it carved by myself. I had whetted the axe only an hour before. It still sparkled in the candlelight.

'I come to bury Caesar, not to praise him,' I said, quoting from a playwright whose name I can't remember.

The pair laughed nervously and Firebrace said he hadn't paid for any extra entertainment.

'Then you can pay for it now,' said I, stepping down and swinging at him with my axe. I missed on purpose, but it gave them a chance to see how sharp the thing was, as it sliced the bed in half.

'Please continue with your pleasure.' I waved my hand in a gracious gesture.

Scroggs reached up to ring the bell, but I chopped the cord and one of his thumbs as he did so. I have never seen so much bobbing and screaming over a minor injury.

Firebrace, not in the least loyal, but most like to Brutus in his treachery, tried to escape through the window, but I soon had his leg off and left him hopping in circles and begging for mercy.

I pulled off my mask and let them see me.

'Preacher Scroggs, on to the block if you will.'

He would not, and I was forced to hold him there myself while I tied him to the rings I had thoughtfully provided in case of such cowardly manners.

'Think of the King,' I said, 'who lay on the block as a lamb to slaughter and never uttered a word.'

Then, without more ado, because I am not a torturer, I took his head off in one clean blow and kicked him off the block.

By this time Firebrace was whimpering in a corner and had soiled his toga with excrement.

'What a sight,' I sneered. 'Are you weeping for your leg? I will bring it and reunite it with your body.'

I fetched his leg from by the window and offered it to him, but he only lamented more loudly and begged me to spare him.

'I may not spare you,' I said. 'For I would rather spare all those who would come into contact with you, were you to be left alive.'

Then I picked him up by the neck, the way a terrier does a rat, and dropped him senseless on the block. That he was unconscious was better for him, my axe having lost its edge so that I was obliged to use two strokes before I could fully sever the head.

My work finished I opened the door, and an eager crowd of good gentlemen poured in, anxious to disport themselves amongst these ruins.

I looked back and saw that one already had Scroggs on the remains of the bed. He was mounting him from behind, all the while furiously kissing the severed head.

I went to the pump where I had once washed myself and all my clothes in favour of love, and I took off what I was wearing and doused myself properly. I wanted no trace of that ungodly pair. When I was clean I walked home naked and burned my clothes in a quiet fire. No one saw me. Like the angels, I can be invisible when there is work to be done.

THE NATURE OF TIME

My experience of time is mostly like my experience with maps. Flat, moving in a more or less straight line from one point to another. Being in time, in a continuous present, is to look at a map and not see the hills, shapes and undulations, but only the flat form. There is no sense of dimension, only a feeling for the surface. Thinking about time is more dizzy and precipitous.

Thinking about time is like turning the globe round and round, recognizing that all journeys exist simultaneously, that to be in one place is not to deny the existence of another, even though that other place cannot be felt or seen, our usual criteria for belief.

Thinking about time is to acknowledge two contradictory certainties: that our outward lives are governed by the seasons and the clock; that our inward lives are governed by something much less regular — an imaginative impulse cutting through the dictates of daily time, and leaving us free to ignore the boundaries of here and now and pass like lightning along the coil of pure time, that is, the circle of the universe and whatever it does or does not contain.

Outside of the rules of daily time, not to be is as exact as to be. We can't talk about all that the universe contains because to do so would be to render it finite and we know in some way, that we cannot prove, that it is infinite. So what the universe doesn't contain is as significant to us as what it does. There will be a moment (though of course it won't be a moment) when we will know (though knowing will no longer be separate from being) that we are a part of all we have met and that all we have met was already a part of us.

Until now religion has described it better than science, but now physics and metaphysics appear to be saying the same thing. The world is flat and round, is it not? We have dreams of moving back and forward in time, though to use the words back and forward is to make a nonsense of the dream, for it implies that time is linear, and if that were so there could be no movement, only a forward progression. But we do not move through time, time moves through us. I say this because our physical bodies have a natural decay span, they are one-use-only units that crumble around us. To everyone, this is a surprise. Although we see it in parents and our friends we are always amazed to see it in ourselves. The most prosaic of us betray a belief in the inward life every time we talk about 'my body' rather than 'I'. We feel it as absolutely part but not at all part of who we are. Language always betrays us, tells the truth when we want to lie, and dissolves into formlessness when we would most like to be precise. And so we cannot move back and forth in time, but we can experience it in a different way. If all time is eternally present, there is no reason why we should not step out of one present into another.

The inward life tells us that we are multiple not single, and that our one existence is really countless existences holding hands like those cut-out paper dolls, but unlike the dolls never coming to an end. When we say, 'I have been here before,' perhaps we mean, 'I am here now,' but in another life, another time, doing something else. Our lives could be stacked together like plates on a waiter's hand. Only the top is showing, but the rest are there and by mistake we discover them.

Our inward life of pure time is sluggish or fast-flowing depending on our rate of conductivity. Just as certain metals and alloys when suitably cooled conduct electricity without generating any heat, and therefore without losing any of the energy they are carrying, so certain people may be superconductors for time. As well as experiencing time as we normally understand it, they may experience time as a larger, all encompassing dimension and so be in touch with much more than the present. Artists and gurus are, in the language of science, superconductors.

Our rate of conductivity is probably determined by an ability, learned or innate, to make the foreground into the background, so that the distractions of the everyday no longer take up our energy. Monks and contemplatives have tried to achieve this by withdrawing from the world – utter concentration, trance-like concentration, is what is needed. Passion, delirium, meditation, even out-of-body, are words we use to describe the heightened condition of superconductivity. It is certainly true that a criterion for true art, as opposed to its cunning counterfeit, is its ability to take us where the artist has been, to this other different place where we are free from the problems of gravity. When we are drawn into the art we are drawn out of ourselves. We are no longer bound by matter, matter has become what it is: empty space and light.

Empty space and light. For us, empty space is space empty of people. The sea blue-black at night, stretched on a curve under the curve of the sky, blue-black and pinned with silver stars that never need polish. The Arctic, where the white snow is the white of nothing and defies the focus of the eye. Forests and rain forests and waterfalls that roar down the hollows of rocks. Deserts like a burning fire. Paintings show us how light affects us, for to live in light is to live in time and not be conscious of it, except in the most obvious ways. Paintings are light caught and held like a genie in jar. The energy is trapped for ever, concentrated, unable to disperse.

Still life is dancing life. The dancing life of light.

Paintings 1 : 'A Hunt in a Forest'. A forest at night. Men in coloured tunics are riding fierce horses. Dogs bark. Disappearing distance into distance into distance the riders get smaller and vanish. Uccello. The coming of perspective.

When I saw this painting I began by concentrating on the foreground figures, and only by degrees did I notice the others, some so faint as to be hardly noticeable.

My own life is like this, or, I should say, my own lives. For the most part I can see only the most obvious detail, the present, my present. But sometimes, by a trick of the light, I can see more than that. I can see countless lives existing together and receding slowly into the trees.

Time 4 : Did my childhood happen? I must believe it did, but I don't have any proof. My mother says it did, but she is a fantasist, a liar and a murderer, though none of that would stop me loving her. I remember things, but I too am a fantasist and a liar, though I have not killed anyone yet.

There are others whom I could ask, but I would not count their word in a court of law. Can I count it in a more serious matter? I will have to assume that I had a childhood, but I cannot assume to have had the one I remember.

Everyone remembers things which never happened. And it is common knowledge that people often forget things which did. Either we are all fantasists and liars or the past has nothing definite in it. I have heard people say we are shaped by our childhood. But which one?

I was walking around the island today when I found a deep pit full of worn-out ballet shoes. The satin was stained and the toes were scuffed through in holes. I followed the track which led from the pit up a short hill and along a ridge thick with blue stone. I soon came to a handsome house, quite out of keeping with the wild surroundings. I pulled on the doorbell but no one answered. Determined now to seek an end to my mystery, I climbed up the side of the house and managed to get through a double window on the top floor. Inside, the rooms were wooden-floored and without furnishings, though each had a large fireplace and in each fireplace a cast of embers or a furious blaze warmed the room.

After some time I heard a sound like music, but not like any music I had heard, and I tracked the noise to a pair of doors which seemed to be bolted. Above the door was a glass pane, and by careful scrambling I was able to balance on the door knobs and peer into the room.

What I saw astonished me.

There appeared to be ten points of light spiralling in a line along the floor, and from these beings came the sound I had heard. It was harmonic but it had no tune. I could hardly bear to look at the light, and the tone, though far from unpleasant, hurt my ears. It was too rich, too strong, to be music.

Then I saw a young woman, darting in a figure of eight in between the lights and turning her hands through it as a potter turns clay on the wheel. At last she stood back, and one by one I watched the light form into a head and arms and legs. Slower and slower, the sound dying with the light, until on the floor were ten women, their shoes in holes, their bodies wet with sweat.

I fell off the door knobs.

When I came to I was in a much smaller room, propped in a chair on one side of the fire. Opposite me, attentive and smiling, was the woman I had first seen at dinner, what seemed like years ago and might have been days.

'My name is Jordan,' I said.

Memory 1 : The scene I have just described to you may lie in the future or the past. Either I have found Fortunata or I will find her. I cannot be sure. Either I am remembering her or I am still imagining her. But she is somewhere in the grid of time, a co-ordinate, as I am.

'My name is Fortunata,' she said. 'This is the first thing I saw.

93

It was winter. The ground was hard and white. There were late roses in the hedges, wild and red, and the holly tree was dark green with blazing berries. It snowed every day, dense curtains of snow that wiped out the footprints coming to and from the house, leaving us to believe that no one ever came here or ever had. One day a robin landed on my windowsill and sank immediately. I dug it out with a teaspoon and it flew away, the snow falling like fetters from its wings. Because the snow was so deep it muffled the noise we made, and we crept about like a silent order, exchanging glances and surprising one another in the garden, where we moved in slow motion, each step shifting feet of snow like sand-dunes.

'As it grew colder and the snow hardened we carved statues from it, scenes from the Bible and the Greek heroes.

'It was the winter of our marriage, my sisters and I. We were to be married all together, all twelve of us on the same day. On New Year's Day, in blood-red dresses with our black hair.

'We decided to build a church in our garden. We built it out of the ice, and it cut our hands and the blood stained the snow like the wild red roses in the hedges. We worked without speaking, only pausing twice a day for meals and lighting up the dark with flares so that we could continue in spite of the shortness of the hours. It was finished the day before the ceremonies. The night before, our last night together as sisters, we slept as always in a long line of single beds beneath the white sheets and blankets like those who have fallen asleep in the snow. From this room, in the past, we had flown to a silver city that knew neither day nor night, and in that city we had danced for joy thinking nothing of the dawn where we lived.

'When it was dawn on our wedding day we dressed in our red dresses and unplaited our hair, and when we were ready we closed and locked the great windows that had been our means of escape and walked in single file from our bedroom down the marble staircase to the frozen church. We were married one by one under branches of mistletoe, but when it came to my turn, and I was the last, I looked at my husband to be, the youngest prince, who had followed us in secret and found us out, and I did not want him.

'At the last possible moment I pushed him aside and ran out of the church through the crowds of guests, mouths open like fishes.

'I took a boat and sailed round the world earning my living as a dancer. Eventually I came here and built this school. I never advertise. People find me because they want to, as you have.'

'I have met your sisters,' I said, and told her how they were all living together again in one place, and related the story of their various divorces.

'But the story they told me about you was not the same. That you escaped, yes, but that you flew away and walked on a wire stretched from the steeple of the church to the mast of a ship at anchor in the bay.'

She laughed. How could such a thing be possible?

'But,' I said, 'how could it be possible to fly every night from the window to an enchanted city when there are no such places?'

'Are there not such places?' she said, and I fell silent, not knowing how to answer.

Lies 8 : It was not the first thing she saw, how could it have been? Nor was the night in the fog-covered field the first thing I saw. But before then we were like those who dream and pass through life as a series of shadows. And so what we have told you is true, although it is not.

Before the great snows and the fields of ice of which I have told you, my sisters and I flew through the window night after night and danced in a silver city of curious motion. The city itself danced. It had the sensation of being on board ship, of being heaved from corner to corner on top of the tossing tide.

To begin with no one in the city danced. They paid their taxes and brought up their children and ate and slept like the rest of the world. But that was when the city was also like the rest of this world, and seemed to be still. Of course, some of the cleverer people knew that the world is endlessly in motion, but since they could not feel it they ignored it.

In the middle of summer, when the dying sun bled the blue sky orange, the movement began. At first it was no more than a termor, then an upheaval, and everyone ran to put their silver in boxes and to tie up the dog.

During the night the shifting continued, and although no one was hurt the doctor of the place issued a written warning to the effect that anyone whose teeth were false should remove them in case of sudden choking. The prudent applied this to hairpieces and false limbs and soon the vaults of the town hall were filled with spare human matter.

As the weeks went by, and it became clear that the underground activity had neither ceased nor worsened, a few brave citizens tried to make the best of it and strung ropes from one point to another, as supports to allow them to go about their business. In time all of the people started to adjust to their new rolling circumstances and it was discovered that the best way to overcome the problem was to balance above it. The ropes were no longer used as supports but as walkways and roads, and everyone, even those who had piled up their limbs in the town hall, learned to be acrobats. Carrying coloured umbrellas to help them balance, they walked in soft shoes from their homes to their usual haunts.

A few generations passed, and no one remembered that the city had ever been like any other, or that the ground was a more habitual residence. Houses were built in the treetops and the birds, disgusted by this invasion of their privacy, swept even higher, cawing and chirping from the banks of clouds.

As it became natural for the citizens to spend their lives suspended, the walking turned to leaping, and leaping into dancing, so that no one bothered to go sedately where they could twist in points of light.

Then there was an accident.

A young girl coming home along a slippery and frayed line of rope missed her footing and fell into the blank space below.

There was a cry of horror from everyone who saw it, but the girl did not drop and crack on the ground, she floated.

After a few simple experiments it became certain that for the people who had abandoned gravity, gravity had abandoned them. There was a general rejoicing, and from that day forth no one concerned themselves with floors or with falling, though it was still thought necessary to build a ceiling in your house in order to place the chandelier.

Now I have told you the history of the city, which is a logical one, each piece fitting into the other without strain. Sure that you must believe something so credible I will continue with the story of our nightly arrival in that city and the sad means of our discovery . . .

The city, being freed from the laws of gravity, began to drift upwards for some 200 miles, until it was out of the earth's atmosphere. It lay for a while above Africa and then began to circle the earth at leisure, never in one place for long, but in other respects like some off-shore island. The citizens had enormous poles made to push themselves off from stars or meteors, and in this way used their town as a raft to travel where they wanted. They did not know it, but when every person pushed with their pole the force created a counterforce, a kind of vacuum that sucked up anything in its wake. The force was very powerful, and all over the world there are stories of entire picnics that have disappeared from checked tablecloths, and small children who have never been seen again.

The citizens always took kindly to whatever their movement sucked up, and ate the food and looked after the children and sailed on.

My sisters and I have always been light. When my third sister was born she was prevented from banging her head against the ceiling only by the umbilical cord. Without that she would have come from the womb and ascended straight upwards.

My fifth sister was so light that she rode on the back of our house cat until she was twelve.

Of course, we were fattened up and given heavy clothing to

wear, but our ballgowns were not heavy, and when we danced we were the envy of all the rest because our feet seemed never to touch the floor. Fortunately our dresses were long, and so no one caught sight of us, floating.

And so, when the weightless city was directly overhead, though utterly concealed, we were the first to feel the pull of it counter-force, and on the same night we found ourselves being dragged out of bed and slammed up against the window like a dozen flies.

We held council amongst ourselves about what to do, and we decided that there were only two possibilities: either we could ballast ourselves against further attack, or we could open ourselves to whatever might happen. Our vote was unanimous, and on the following night we lay in bed in our ballgowns and waited.

At about one in the morning, when my father's snores were rattling the house, our windows flew open and we were pulled through them, hanging on to each other by our plaits. In an instant we had reached the city, and after our initial surprise we joined in the dancing and the merriment until dawn.

It was then that we encountered our first and only difficulty.

How were we to get back?

After various unprofitable discussions I remembered how Cyrano de Bergerac had attempted to launch himself at the moon by clinging on to the kind of metal that the moon attracted to herself, being magnetic. It seemed to me that the earth, weighed down as it is by gravity, would most likely attract lead to itself, and with this in mind we filled our boots with it and sat upon a sheet of it like a doleful magic carpet. We then bade the people cast us off, which they did with many tears, feeling sure that we would never be seen again.

They were wrong. The lead worked perfectly and we landed on the church roof at the back of our own home. From there it was an easy climb between the chimney stacks, down the wisteria and into bed.

Our happiness continued night after night until my father noticed our pale faces and tired eyes and set a watch on us. But we were cunning and always drugged whoever was on duty, and continued as before. Imagine our horror, then, when my father announced that anyone able to tell where it was we went at night would be rewarded by any one of us in marriage.

Not surprisingly, princes came from every land, and most of them were easy to fool, and we grew too confident.

Our end came in this way.

The people of the floating city had told us it was time for them to anchor in some other place, and asked if we would like to live with them forever. We agreed that we would, and it was arranged that after a night of celebration we would slip home, collect a few possessions and return in time to drift through space for ever. It was the night of the youngest prince, a cunning fellow who guessed at our sleeping draught and who clung to our skirts when we flew away. He was light and invisible and hid between the lanterns and the trees, and no one saw him. When we travelled home on our sheet of lead he was clinging to the underside like a beetle.

The following night, as we were ready to leave and all was happiness, the doors of our chamber burst open and my father came in lit by torches and surrounded by servants.

There was no escape and, to contain us, our ankles were chained and the prince came to stay with his eleven brothers.

Very often in the days that followed we looked at the sky and thought where we might be and knew where we were.

And the rest of the story you know.

I stayed with Fortunata for one month, learning more about her ways and something about my own. She told me that for years she had lived in hope of being rescued; of belonging to someone else, of dancing together. And then she had learned to dance alone, for its own sake and for hers.

'And love?' I said.

She spread her hands and gave me a short lecture on the habits of the starfish.

It was later that I took my medallion from round my neck and put it over her head. She turned it up towards her and read the inscription. 'Remember the rock from whence ye are hewn and the pit from whence ye are digged.'

She laughed. 'What about your wings?' she said. 'How can you forget those when the stumps are still deep in your shoulder-blades?'

I didn't say anything. In the Bible only the angels have wings; the rest of us have to wait to be rescued.

Paintings 2 : 'St Nicholas Calming the Tempest'. A small boat on a blue-black sea. The tempest rages and the four disciples huddle together in fear. Beneath the boat is a great fish, and up above, in full dress and mitre, comes St Nicholas flying through the sky. The stars hang about him.

I am getting ready to leave. Fortunata will not come with me and I cannot stay here, though part of me also belongs to the wilderness. I thought she might want to travel but she tells me truths I already know, that she need not leave this island to see the world, she has seas and cities enough in her mind. If she does, if we all do, it may be that this world and the moon and stars are also a matter of the mind, though a mind of vaster scope than ours. If someone is thinking me, then I am still free to come and go. It will not be like chess, this thoughtful universe, it will be a theatre of changing sets, where we could walk through walls if we wanted, but do not, being faithful to our own sense of the dramatic.

When I was little my mother took me to see a great wonder. It was about 1633, I think, and never before had there been a banana in England. I saw it held high above a man's head. It was yellow and speckled brown, and as I looked at it I saw the tree and the beach and the white waves below birds with wide wings. Then I forgot it completely. But in my games with ships and plants I was trying to return to that memory, to release whatever it had begun in me.

When Tradescant asked me to go with him as an explorer I thought I might be a hero after all, and bring back something that mattered, and in the process find something I had lost.

The sense of loss was hard to talk about. What could I have lost when I never had anything to begin with?

I had myself to begin with, and that is what I lost. Lost it in my mother because she is bigger and stronger than me and that's not how it's supposed to be with sons. But lost it more importantly in the gap between my ideal of myself and my pounding heart.

I want to be brave and admired and have a beautiful wife and a fine house. I want to be a hero and wave goodbye to my wife and children at the docks, and be sorry to see them go but more excited about what is to come. I want to be like other men, one of the boys, a back-slapper and a man who knows a joke or two. I want to be like my rip-roaring mother who cares nothing for how she looks, only for what she does. She has never been in love, no, and never wanted to be either. She is self-sufficient and without self-doubt. Before I left I took her down the Thames and out to sea but I don't know if it made any impression on her, or even how much she noticed. We never talked much. She is silent, the way men are supposed to be. I often caught her staring at me as though she had never seen me before; she seemed to be learning me. I think she loves me but I don't know. She wouldn't say so; perhaps she doesn't know herself. When I left, I think it was relief she felt at being able to continue her old life with the dogs and the dredgers and the whores she likes. Even while Tradescant was talking about it she got up and went for a walk. She was busy with her own mind, but I was hurt.

We never discussed whether or not I would go; she took it for granted, almost as though she had expected it. I wanted her to ask me to stay, just as now I want Fortunata to ask me to stay.

Why do they not?

For Tradescant being a hero comes naturally. His father was a hero before him. The journeys he makes can be tracked on any map and he knows what he's looking for. He wants to bring back rarities and he does.

Our ship, which is weighing anchor some miles from this island, is full of fruit and spices and new plants. When we get home, men and women will crowd round us and ask us what happened and every version we tell will be a little more fanciful. But it will be real, whereas if I begin to tell my story about where I've been or where I think I've been, who will believe me? In a boy it might be indulged, but I'm not a boy any more, I'm a man.

I've kept the log book for the ship. Meticulously. And I've kept a book of my own, and for every journey we have made together I've written down my own journey and drawn my own map. I can't show this to the others, but I believe it to be a faithful account of what happened, at least, of what happened to me.

Are we all living like this? Two lives, the ideal outer life and the inner imaginative life where we keep our secrets?

Curiously, the further I have pursued my voyages the more distant they have become. For Tradescant, voyages can be completed. They occupy time comfortably. With some leeway, they are predictable. I have set off and found that there is no end to even the simplest journey of the mind. I begin, and straight away a hundred alternative routes present themselves. I choose one, no sooner begin, than a hundred more appear. Every time I try to narrow down my intent I expand it, and yet those straits and canals still lead me to the open sea, and then I realize how vast it all is, this matter of the mind. I am confounded by the shining water and the size of the world.

The Buddhists say there are 149 ways to God. I'm not looking for God, only for myself, and that is far more complicated. God has a great deal written about Him; nothing has been written about me. God is bigger, like my mother, easier to find, even in the dark. I could be anywhere, and since I can't describe myself I can't ask for help. We are alone in this quest, and Fortunata is right not to disguise it, though she may be wrong about love. I have met a great many pilgrims on their way towards God and I wonder why they have chosen to look for him rather than themselves. Perhaps I'm missing the point – perhaps whilst looking for someone else you might come across yourself unexpectedly, in a garden somewhere or on a mountain watching the rain. But they don't seem to care about who they are. Some of them have told me that the very point of searching for God is to forget about oneself, to lose oneself for ever. But it is not difficult to lose oneself, or is it the ego they are talking about, the hollow, screaming cadaver that has no spirit within it?

I think that cadaver is only the ideal self run mad, and if the other life, the secret life, could be found and brought home, then a person might live in peace and have no need for God. After all, He has no need for us, being complete.

I have packed my striped bag and taken my coat from the hook where Fortunata put it. She has come to see me off and we are standing together by my boat, which is still staggered with rocks in a high hollow.

Her hair is down, it reaches almost to her waist. She looks serene.

'I'll come back another day,' I say.

She smiles at me and says nothing, and even as I say it I know it won't be true. She will elude me, she and this island will slip sideways in time and I'll never find them again, except perhaps in a dream.

I throw my things into the boat and shove my shoulder against it and push it out into the water. Far away, a black dot is Tradescant's ship. He won't wait much longer.

She wades into the water with me, deep enough to wet the bottom of her hair, and takes my face in both her hands and kisses me on the mouth. Then she turns away and I watch her walk back across the sand and up over the rocks. I begin to row, using her body as a marker.

I always will.

The pineapple arrived today.

Jordan carried it in his arms as though it were a yellow baby; with the wisdom of Solomon he prepared to slice it in two. He had not sharpened the knife before Mr Rose, the royal gardener, flung himself across the table and begged to be sawn into bits instead. Those at the feast contorted themselves with laughter, and the King himself, in his new wig, came down from the dais and urged Mr Rose to delay his sacrifice. It was, after all, only a fruit. At this Mr Rose poked up his head from his abandonment amongst the dishes and reminded the company that this was an historic occasion. Indeed it was. It was 1661, and from Jordan's voyage to Barbados the first pineapple had come to England.

Tradescant is dead. Cromwell is dead. Ireton and Bradshaw, the King's prosecutors, frequently found together beneath soiled sheets, are dead. Jordan missed a pretty sight, sailing too late with his yellow cargo. Cromwell, Ireton and Bradshaw, who had thought to lie peacefully in Westminster Abbey, that place of sanctity they had denied their rightful King, were dug out on 30 January and hung up for all to see on the gallows at Tyburn. That was a moment for a scented handkerchief. Not everyone has as strong a constitution as myself. Thousands of us flocked to watch them swinging in the wind, what was left of them, decay having made no exception for their eminence. The people were mightily pleased to see the thing and a number of stalls sprang up right beneath the bony feet, selling apples and hot biscuits. A gypsy with a crown of stars offered to tell fortunes, but when she looked at my hand she looked away. I was not discouraged; I am enough to make my own fortune in this pock-marked world.

It did render me philosophical though, to sit at Tyburn and watch the merriment and the great wonder of passers-by, especially small children, who had never thought what it might mean to rot.

And yet rotting is a common experience. We all shall, even myself, though I imagine it will take a worm of some endeavour to make any impression.

Firebrace and Scroggs are dead. The sisters at the Spital-fields brothel made a great profit that night, when the word was passed round that there were freshly dismembered bodies to be had. The brothel is gone now, my friend dead from disease and the other sisters vanished the way women do.

I miss Tradescant. He left me a viper in a bottle before he died, to remind me of happier times when we waged war on all vipers. I wish he could see this mess on ropes, it would gladden him to think there is still justice in the world.

My neighbour the witch is not dead. She is much shrunken, even more than she was when Jordan was found. She is about the height of a beagle, with great eyes and ears to match. Her house was lost over the years, in one skirmish or another, but I have lent her a dog kennel till the end of her days. She has done nothing to deserve my charity, but it is my undoing and my cross to bear. She still claims to predict the future and is often to be found brooding over my watercress bed, observing the shifting pattern of the teeth.

When Tradescant died, Jordan took over the expeditions and charted the courses and decided what was precious and what was not. He's been at sea for thirteen years, though I've had gifts from him and I've always known that he would come back . . .

At sunset, on the day of the gibbet, soldiers of the new King, our own Charles the Second, came and took down the bodies and threw them in the common pit beneath the gallows, a stinking place already full of rank and sweating corpses. The heads of the three were chopped off and mounted on the top of Westminster Abbey, a piece of theatre that greatly improved the tempers of all going to and fro.

As for the rest of the forty-nine who had signed the King's death warrant, forty-one were still alive in 1660 when the new King returned. I have always thought us too civilized a nation, though I have a soft heart myself, and I was sorry to see that only nine of those forty-one received the proper penalty under the law for their unanimous murder.

These nine, close associates of Cromwell, were half hanged, then disembowelled and quartered while still alive. If they showed signs of fainting from their ordeal they were thoroughly roused with vinegar and oil of cloves or occasionally a bucket of rancid water. I had been hoping to catch a bit of bowel or any innard as a souvenir for Jordan, but when I darted forward with my bag I was told that all remains were the property of the Crown. If Tradescant had been alive he would have intervened. As it was I made do with seeing and remembering, and at night-time I was fortunate enough to find a gall bladder complete with several stones. I have it by the viper next to my bed.

Whilst Jordan was away I discovered from my time in the brothel that men's members, if bitten off or otherwise severed, do not grow again. This seems a great mistake on the part of nature, since men are so careless with their members and will put them anywhere without thinking. I believe they would force them in a hole in the wall if no better could be found.

I did mate with a man, but cannot say that I felt anything at all, though I had him jammed up to the hilt. As for him, spread on top of me with his face buried beneath my breasts, he complained that he could not find the sides of my cunt and felt like a tadpole in a pot. He was an educated man and urged me to try and squeeze in my muscles, and so perhaps bring me closer to his prong. I took a great breath and squeezed with all my might and heard something like a rush of air through a tunnel, and when I strained up on my elbows and looked down I saw I had pulled him in, balls and everything. He was stuck. I had the presence of mind to ring the bell and my friend came in with her sisters, and with the aid of a crowbar they prised him out and refreshed him with mulled wine while I

106

sang him a little song about the fortitude of spawning salmon. He was a gallant gentleman and offered a different way of pleasuring me, since I was the first woman he said he had failed. Accordingly, he burrowed down the way ferrets do and tried to take me in his mouth. I was very comfortable about this, having nothing to be bitten off. But in a moment he thrust up his head and eyed me wearily.

'Madam,' he said, 'I am sorry. I beg your pardon but I cannot.'

'Cannot?'

'Cannot. I cannot take that orange in my mouth. It will not fit. Neither can I run my tongue over it. You are too big, madam.'

I did not know what part of me he was describing, but I felt pity for him and offered him more wine and some pleasant chat.

When he had gone I squatted backwards on a pillow and parted my bush of hair to see what it was that had confounded him so. It seemed all in proportion to me. These gentlemen are very timid.

When I was a girl I heard my mother and father copulating. I heard my father's steady grunts and my mother's silence. Later my mother told me that men take pleasure and women give it. She told me in a matter-of-fact way, in the same tone of voice she used to tell me how to feed the dogs or make bread.

When I was born I was tiny enough to sleep in my father's shoe; it was only later that I began to grow, and to grow to such proportions that my father had the idea of exhibiting me. My mother refused him, saying no member of her family should be the subject of an exhibition, no matter how poor we became. One night my father tried to steal me and sell me to a man with one leg. They had a barrel ready to put me in, but no sooner had they slammed on the lid than I burst the bonds of the barrel and came flying out at my father's throat.

This was my first murder.

I have forgotten my childhood, not just because of my

father but because it was a bleak and unnecessary time, full of longing and lost hope. I can remember some incidents, but the sense of time passing escapes me. If I were to stretch out all that seemed to happen, and relive it, it might take a day or two. Where then are all the years in between?

When I got news of Jordan's return I knew he would be returning as a hero and that I had to meet him as a hero's mother. I spared no expense and had a new dress made of the finest wool with a beautiful shawl cut out of the altar cloth of Stepney church. I made the journey to Hove in a carriage and set up my encampment on the beach, waiting for the first sign of Jordan's sail. When he left me he was nineteen, with crow-black hair and a quiet voice. He was thirty-three now, and I could not picture him.

There were the usual villains on the sands, hoping to rob a poor woman in her sleep, but I pushed them under-water and left them bloated with salt. In my spare time I collected shells.

At last, on the third day, I saw a speck at sea. It grew bigger as the hours passed and by evening I could see it in full sail anchoring. I put my hands to my mouth and shouted Jordan's name, not being able to tell if he could hear me above the screaming of the gulls dropping for fish.

I lit my fire and waited. In the darkness Jordan let down a small boat and put a lantern in the prow. He rowed towards me so softly that it wasn't until I heard him jump out knee-deep in the water that I looked up and ran to help him pull up the boat.

His beard was grey in parts. He smiled at me and took a wash-leather bag from his pocket. There was a rope of pearls inside. I put them on and they glinted in the firelight. He had a pan with him, and some food, and still without speaking we sat opposite one another over the fire, the black sails of the ship visible in the moonlight, his boat dark on the sands.

I wanted to tell him things, to tell him I loved him and how much I'd missed him, but thirteen years of words were fighting in my throat and I couldn't get any of them out. There was too much to say so I said nothing.

We ate our food and I sat with my knees drawn up, my

back against a rock, while he lay on his side, his legs out, his body propped on one elbow. He was watching the waves.

When he fell asleep I crept across to cover him up with my blankets and I looked at the length of him, his thin wrists and nose like a sharp slope. I stroked his hair and I realized his face was scarred. No one would hurt him now. As I pulled the cover up to his chin I noticed something glinting round his neck. Gently, so as not to wake him, I untangled it from his clothing and saw it to be a silver pendant. I had not given it to him. It was not his medallion. It was a tiny pair of shoes, dancing shoes, their feet curved inwards as though standing on tip-toe. He turned suddenly and grunted, and as I let go of the chain he took it in one hand rather as a child will hold its mother's thumb.

I lifted his head and put my shawl beneath it, and sat all night at his feet, counting the hours by the tide.

SOME YEARS LATER

PAINTINGS 3 : 'Mr Rose, the Royal Gardener, presents the pineapple to Charles the Second'. The artist is unknown, probably Dutch. Mr Rose in his wig is down on one knee and the King in his wig is accepting the pineapple. Colours of fruit and flowers make up the painting.

Soon after I saw this painting I decided to join the Navy. My father was pleased, my mother was worried. I was straight out of school and eager for a career. Any career that would take me away.

Three things coincided.

I saw the painting and tried to imagine what it would be like to bring something home for the first time. I tried to look at a pineapple and pretend I'd never seen one before. I couldn't do it. There's so little wonder left in the world because we've seen everything one way or another. Where had that pineapple come from? Barbados was easy to find out, but who had brought it, and under what circumstances, and why?

I bought a pineapple and kept it in my room until it went rotten. My mother kept coming in and putting her nose to the air like a Pointer.

She said, 'I can smell something, you know.'

Later she said, 'I can smell something sweet.'

Then, 'There's something rotting in here.'

She found it under the bed and threw it away. It was pulpy inside, and the skin had shrivelled into scaly geometric shapes.

Before she found it – and I kept it a long time, thanks to the common methods of injecting preservative into whatever's alive – I used to take it out at night and feel its sprouting head and rough body. If I thought she wouldn't come in early in the morning I chanced sleeping with it, though on those days she complained I smelled of fruit.

113

'How can the boy smell of fruit?' said my father. 'He hasn't been near any fruit.'

I dropped my head and finished my porridge obediently. My mother has often been labelled as strange but that's because she says things people can't possibly believe. Mostly she's right.

I said to my friend Jack, 'Jack, don't you wish we could still be pirates or something?'

He said, 'Don't be stupid, Nicolas, all that water and no soap.'

He's very clean, Jack.

Nicolas Jordan. Five foot ten. Dark. Makes model boats and sails them at the weekend. Best friend Jack. No brothers or sisters. Parents can't afford a telescope. Has a book instead on how to navigate by the stars, and a pair of binoculars on a khaki strap. That's all there is to say about me. On the outside, anyway.

The second of the three things was *The Observer's Book of Ships*. I bought it in a second-hand shop. The frontispiece said:

By

Frank E. Dodman

foreworded by

A.C. Hardy BSc, MINA, FRGS

For a long time I had a secret lover called Mina Frogs. When I came home a hero she was always waiting at the docks and desperate to marry me. I loved that book, describing over a hundred types of ships with ninety-five line drawings, sixteen colour plates and sixteen pages of photographs.

I built my own model ship from the pictures. At first I had kits with balsa wood rigging and plastic seamen, but soon I learned to design my own with tools from my father's workshop. I never bothered with a crew. The crew weren't beautiful, they were just slaves of the ship.

At weekends my mother cooked and my father read the paper. I went to the pond and sailed my boats. I liked the uncertainty of the wind. Jack came with me, bringing his books on computer science and his father's copies of *GP*, a magazine for doctors. The magazines were full of pictures of incurables, and that included anyone suffering from the common cold.

'It has to go away of its own accord,' said Jack. 'All those little pills are just money-makers.'

'Like love,' I said, setting the rudder. 'There's no cure for love.'

'Who are you in love with?' said Jack.

'No one. She doesn't exist.'

'It's the most unhygienic thing you can do,' said Jack.

'It can't be. What about people who work in sewers?'

'They wear protective clothing. People in love hardly ever wear clothes – look at the magazines.'

He meant *Playboy* and *Penthouse*. His father took those too.

I ignored him then and let him get back to his books. He loved computers, so clean, so programmable. When I told him I had learned to steer by the stars, he said, 'What for?'

He isn't insensitive, he's just modern.

One afternoon, when Jack was lying on his side reading about how some kids had broken into the computer at the Pentagon, a man came over to me and rested on his heels by my boat.

'You made it yourself?'

'Yes.'

'What kit?'

'No kit. I made it, that's all.'

'Can she sail?'

'Oh yes. I've balanced her perfectly. She's ready for any wind.'

'I used to make them,' said the man, 'and sail in them too. I've been everywhere, but I still have a feeling I've missed it. I feel like I'm being laughed at, I don't know what by, who by, it sounds silly. I think I may have missed the world, that the one I've seen is a decoy to get me off the scent. I feel as though I'm always on the brink of making sense of it and then I lose it again.'

He stood up; he didn't look at me. Then he walked away.

I picked up my boat and went over to Jack.

'Who was that?' he said.

'I don't know. A sailor or someone.'

'He must be a nut.'

'Why?'

'Nobody wears clothes like that any more.'

'Come on Jack. I'm hungry.'

And the third thing?

I was cleaning out my bedroom. We were decorating the house. Under the bed were stacks of books I'd read when I was younger. I put most of them in a box, not even glancing at them. There was one I remembered, remembered so vividly that it came to me not as a thought but as a taste in the mouth. It was rainy when I was reading it, rainy and soon after Christmas. It was called *The Boys' Book of Heroes*, and on the front there were ships and aeroplanes and horses and men with steel jaws. I opened it and some pages fell out in my own childish handwriting. I suppose I had been ten at the time. It was my précis of heroes. The ones I liked. I'd drawn pictures of them in the margin.

William the Conqueror

Born 1028. Known as 'William the Bastard'. Three of his guardians died violent deaths and his tutor was murdered. 'William was an out-of-doors man, a hunter, a soldier, fierce and despotic. Uneducated. He had few graces . . .'

He married Matilda, daughter of Baldwin the Fifth of Flanders. The Pope condemned the marriage and they were forced to build a monastery each as a penance.

As the cousin of the childless Edward the Confessor, William the Bastard had expected to inherit England by right. When Harold got it instead he invaded.

Christopher Columbus

Otherwise known to his Spanish friends as Christobel Colon. He was born in Genoa, the son of a weaver, and he started his seafaring career as a pirate.

He discovered America by prophecy rather than astronomy, writing to King Ferdinand and Queen Isabella of Spain in 1502 that 'neither reason nor mathematics nor maps were of any use to me'. He later wrote his own *Book of Prophecies* and died in obscurity.

Francis Drake

Born in 1540 in Devon, he went to sea at thirteen, and when he was thirty-seven he set off in the *Golden Hind* to sail round the world. He was later made Mayor of Plymouth.

Notable for his defeat of the Armada, he was also Queen Elizabeth's favourite looter and was nicknamed 'the master-thief of the Unknown World'.

The most popular hero for the following 200 years, he was 'short of stature, of strong limb, round headed, brown hair, full bearded, his eyes round and large and clear'.

Lord Nelson

Born in 1758, Nelson went to sea at nine and had been to the Arctic by the time he was fifteen. On another voyage he contracted malaria and had a vision. "'Well, then,' I exclaimed, 'I will be a hero.'"

When Wellington met Nelson he said his talk was 'all about himself and in really a style so vain and silly as to surprise and almost disgust me'. None the less, Nelson took possession of the flagship *Victory* and set off to defeat Napoleon. He outlined his self-confessedly brilliant plan of attack, calling it 'the Nelson touch'.

He was killed in the historic battle but before he died he had signed a document bequeathing his mistress, Emma, Lady Hamilton, and their child, Horatia, to the nation. The nation took no notice and lauded the dead Admiral while Emma died in Calais nine years later, raddled with disease and quite alone.

If you're a hero you can be an idiot, behave badly, ruin your personal life, have any number of mistresses and talk about yourself all the time, and nobody minds. Heroes are immune. They have wide shoulders and plenty of hair and wherever they go a crowd gathers. Mostly they enjoy the company of other men, although attractive women are part of their reward.

My father watches war films. War films are full of men in tin hats talking in terse sentences. They play cards round folding tables and lean over to each other from their bunk beds. They jump out of trenches and mow with their machine guns in 180 arcs. They have girlfriends but they prefer each other.

My father watches submarine films. The siren goes and the men in T-shirts get thrown against the wall. The commander glues himself to the periscope and we get a clip of the submarine going down like a steel whale.

My father watches ocean-going films. Men in polo-neck sweaters and black wellingtons running on to the bridge and asking about the enemy. There's always a little guy with a mop who says simple important things that all the bigger guys ignore. Later in the film, when the ship's going down, the little guy's the only one who's small enough to jam his body in the gaping hole and stop the sea pouring in. He doesn't look like a hero but he is one. He's there to make all the small men feel brave. A lot of small men would like to be heroes, they have to have their fantasy moment. Thing is, the small ones always get killed.

I went to the Navy recruitment office and they told me about all the sophisticated equipment I'd be using and all the places I'd see. They had a film show about life in the Navy and afterwards an old Admiral turned up and told us how he'd learned to iron his bell-bottom trousers with seven creases for the seven seas.

There was a lot about camaraderie and mates. It's not homosexual, of course.

Jack and I went to the park. I had my boat, he had his books. It was windy and the pond looked like grey icing forked over.

I left him on a bench and went down to the gravel edge. I trimmed the sail and got ready to lean my boat into the water. The wind took her right into the middle and bent the rigging sideways. I got her back in the end but she was damaged. The wind made my eyes run and Jack thought I was crying. He was embarrassed and tried to laugh too loud at a woman whose deckchair had blown inside out.

He said, 'You're too old for this boat stuff.'

I said, 'Why am I?'

He shrugged and told me he was getting a Saturday job for the holidays.

My mother and father are very tidy eaters. They arrange their food according to colour and shape and eat proportionally so that they never have too much of one thing and too little of another. I eat all of my peas first and this annoys them.

We have been talking about my career in the Navy.

'What if there's a war?' said my mother.

'You and I were both in the war,' said my father. 'We're all right.'

'It was nerve-racking,' said my mother.

'It wasn't too bad, we had good times — do you remember when we danced together and then made love in the dark?'

'Don't say that in front of Nicolas,' said my mother. Then, after a little pause, 'It was nerve-racking.'

Did she mean the war or making love to my father?

I was accepted as a naval cadet. We were proud when the letter arrived. My mother put it in a folder she has with other things of mine.

The night before I left we had a special dinner and a bottle of wine. My mother was nervous, my father was loud. I tried to leave my peas till last.

At bed-time I went into my room and put out the light. I didn't get undressed. I lay on my bed and looked out of the window at the stars. I read in a book that the stars can take you anywhere. I've never wanted to be an astronaut because

119

of the helmets. If I were up there on the moon, or by the Milky Way, I'd want to feel the stars round my head. I'd want them in my hair the way they are in paintings of the gods. I'd want my whole body to feel the space, the empty space and points of light. That's how dancers must feel, dancers and acrobats, just for a second, that freedom.

Even if you were free from gravity it wouldn't feel good in a space suit. Wouldn't you want to be naked? Naked and turning your body in slow somersaults through a new atmosphere?

People say the magic has gone out of the moon now that someone's stood on it. I don't think so. It would take more than a man's foot to steal the moon.

We've been everywhere in the world and now we've gone into space.

My father watches space films. They're different: they're the only area of undiminished hope. They're happy and they have women in them who are sometimes scientists rather than singers or waitresses. Sometimes the women get to be heroes too, though this is still not as popular. When I watch space films I always want to cry because they leave you with so much to hope for, it feels like a beginning, not a tired old end.

But when we've been everywhere, and it's only a matter of time, where will we go next, when there are no more wildernesses?

Will it take as long as that before we start the journey inside, down our own time tunnels and deep into the realms of inner space?

My bedroom was put away. I had put myself away in cupboards or out of sight. It was a spare room now. I was leaving home. In the light from the window I could see my empty shelves and the shoes I wouldn't need neat in a row under the wardrobe. It was an old wardrobe with a mirror on the inside door. I looked at myself once more in the morning before I left. I looked all right.

Six months later I was on board an admiralty tug in the Thames Estuary outside Deptford. We were after a mine

120

someone had spotted, or said they had. There was no hurry. The public were reassured by our presence and we were reassured by ourselves. It was a warm night, the lights of London and the black water all restful enough. I was content.

I was standing on deck with a friend of mine. He was an astronomer of sorts and liked to show me the constellations. I didn't tell him I already knew them.

Then he said, 'You know, if we were turned loose in our galaxy, just let out there one day by ourselves, it wouldn't look like it does from here. We'd see nothing but blackness. All those stars that hang so close together are light years apart. Our chances of finding any star or planet at all, forget about a blue planet like this one, would be a billion billion.'

He laughed and went below.

I rested my arms on the railing and my head on my arms. I felt I was falling falling into a black hole with no stars and no life and no helmet. I heard a foot scrape on the deck beside me. Then a man's voice said, 'They are burying the King at Windsor today.' snapped upright and looked full in the face of the man, who was staring out over the water. I knew him but from where? And his clothes . . . nobody wears clothes like that any more.

I looked beyond him, upwards. The sails creaked in the breeze, the main spar was heavy with rope. Further beyond I saw the Plough and Orion and the bright sickle of the moon.

I heard a bird cry, sharp and fierce. Tradescant sighed.   My name is Jordan.

I am a woman going mad. I am a woman hallucinating. I imagine I am huge, raw, a giant. When I am a giant I go out with my sleeves rolled up and my skirts swirling round me like a whirlpool. I have a sack such as kittens are drowned in and I stop off all over the world filling it up. Men shoot at me, but I take the bullets out of my cleavage and I chew them up. Then I laugh and laugh and break their guns between my fingers the way you would a wish-bone.

First Stop: the World Bank.

I go straight to the boardroom. There's a long hardwood table surrounded by comfortable chairs. Men in suits are discussing how to deal with the problem of the Third World. They want to build dams, clear the rain forests, finance huge Coca-Cola plants and exploit the rubber potential.

They say, 'This is a private meeting.'

I start at the top end and I pick them up one by one by the scruff of their necks. Their legs wriggle in their Gucci suits; I've got nothing against the suits, lovely material. I drop them into my sack, all screaming at once about calling their lawyers and who do I think I am and what about free speech and civil liberties.

When they're all in the bag, I leave the room tidy, throw in a few calculators so they won't be bored, and off we go.

Next Stop: the Pentagon.

I smash through the maximum security doors, past the computers, the secrets, the army of secretaries, and burst into a band of generals and lesser lights talking about defence and peace and how to eliminate the nuclear threat by ordering more weapons. I listen carefully while they tell me with all the patience of a mother to a defective child that if we don't have enough force to blow up the world fifty times over, we're not safe. If we do, we are.

I say, 'Your own statistics show that, if three per cent of the Defence Budget were spent on the poverty problem in the United States over the next ten years, there would be no problem, you'd wipe it out.'

They look at one another and give little indulgent chuckles and turn back to work. I have no choice. I grab them by their medals and drop them in the bag. One of them pokes his head out of the top and says, 'You should be arrested. What you're doing is dangerous!'

And then . . .

I snatch world leaders from motorcades, from mansion

122

house dinners, from embassies and private parties. I throw them all in the bag and we go on foot to the butter mountains and wine lakes and grain silos and deserts and cracked earth and starving children and arms dealers in guarded palaces.

I force all the fat ones to go on a diet, and all the men line up for compulsory training in feminism and ecology. Then they start on the food surpluses, packing it with their own hands, distributing it in a great human chain of what used to be power and is now co-operation.

We change the world, and on the seventh day we have a party at the wine lake and make pancakes with the butter mountain and the peoples of the earth keep coming in waves and being fed and being clean and being well. And when the rivers sparkle, it's not with mercury . . .

That's how it started, the mercury. That's where my hallucinations began, checking mercury levels in rivers and lakes and streams. Anywhere that profit might have been. The levels were always too high, the fish were dying, children had strange scaly diseases which the government said had no connection with anything whatsoever.

I started a one-woman campaign, the sort you read about in the papers where the woman is thought to be a bit loopy but harmless enough. They hope you'll go away, get older, get bored. Time is a great deadener.

I didn't go away. I wrote articles and pushed fact sheets through front doors. I developed a passion for personal evangelism. I stopped housewives on street corners and working men in caffs. Where women were high-placed I asked for money and help.

The cost to myself was high. Too high, I thought, when I was depressed, which was often. The trouble is that when most people are apathetic ordinary people like me have to go too far, have to ruin their lives and be made an object of scorn just to get the point across. Did they really think I'd rather be camping by a polluted river than sitting in my own flat with my things about me?

People will believe anything.

Except, it seems, the truth.

I was a lonely child. My parents found me difficult, not the child they had wanted. I was too intense, too physically awkward and too quiet for them. My best times were outside with our dogs. Parents want to see themselves passed on in their children. It comforts them to recognize a twist of the head or a way of talking. If there are no points of recognition, if the child is genuinely alien, they do their best to feed and clothe, but they don't love. Not in the transforming way of love.

So I learned to be alone and to take pleasure in the dark where no one could see me and where I could look at the stars and invent a world where there was no gravity, no holding force. I wasn't fat because I was greedy; I hardly ate at all. I was fat because I wanted to be bigger than all the things that were bigger than me. All the things that had power over me. It was a battle I intended to win.

It seems obvious, doesn't it, that someone who is ignored and overlooked will expand to the point where they have to be noticed, even if the noticing is fear and disgust.

I imagined my parents' house as a shell to contain me. An environment suitable for a fantastic creature who needed to suck in the warmth and nourishment until it was ready to shrug off the shell and burst out. At night, in bed, I felt the whole house breathing in and out as I did. The roof tiles, the bricks, the lagging, the plumbing, all were subject to my rhythm. I was a monster in a carpeted egg.

There I go, my shoulders pushing into the corners of the room, my head uncurling and smashing the windows. Shards of glass everywhere, the garden trodden in a single footprint. Micromegas, 200 miles high.

But there is no Rabelaisian dimension for rage.

When I left home, predictably, I lost weight. Wheelbarrows full of weight. Two wheelbarrows, in fact, that's what I worked out. Where did it go? Where does it come from

124

and where does it go? It's one of the mysteries of matter, that fat appears and then disappears again, and all you have to say it ever was are a few stretchmarks and some outsize clothes.

'You'll burn it off,' my mother used to say, and when I was a child I had visions of myself stoking a great furnace with fat. The smoke that came out of the chimney was curly, like pig's tails.

When the weight had gone I found out something strange: that the weight persisted in my mind. I had an *alter ego* who was huge and powerful, a woman whose only morality was her own and whose loyalties were fierce and few. She was my patron saint, the one I called on when I felt myself dwindling away through cracks in the floor or slowly fading in the street. Whenever I called on her I felt my muscles swell and laughter fill up my throat. Of course it was only a fantasy, at least at the beginning . . .

As a chemist with a good degree, and as an attractive woman whom men like to work with, I could have taught in a university or got a job doing worthy work behind the scenes. I needn't have gone into pollution research. It's odious in every way. Big companies hate you and continually set their in-house scientists to discredit your facts. Governments at home and abroad are very slow to notice what you say. Slowness is the best you can hope for, outright hostility and muddling methods are more usual. The earth is being murdered and hardly anyone wants to believe it.

'Why don't you work for ICI?' my father said. 'They've got a share-option scheme.'

Yes, why don't I, or Shell, or Esso, or Union Carbide, or NASA?

Why don't I take the share option and the company car and the pension scheme and the private health care and the reassuring salary? Why am I camping by a river and going mad? My skin is flaking off.

I have been alone for a long time, days and nights of time, so that time is no longer measured in the units I am used to but has mutinied and run wild. I do not measure time now, time measures me.

This is frightening.

Very often I sleep all day and stay awake all night – why should I not, since there is no one to mind?

I have a calendar and a watch, and so rationally I can tell where I am in this thing called a year. My own experience is different. I feel as though I have been here for years already. I could be talked out of that but I couldn't be persuaded not to feel it any more. How do you persuade someone not to feel? And so my strongest instinct is to abandon the common-sense approach and accept what is actually happening to me; that time has slowed down.

Why not? Under certain conditions our pulses slow or race, our breathing alters, the whole body will change its habit if necessary.

There are so many fairy stories about someone who falls asleep for a little while and wakes up to find himself in a different time. Outwardly nothing is changing for me, but inwardly I am not always here, sitting by a rotting river. I can still escape.

Escape from what? The present? Yes, from this foreground that blinds me to whatever may be happening in the distance. If I have a spirit, a soul, any name will do, then it won't be single, it will be multiple. Its dimension will not be one of confinement but one of space. It may inhabit numerous changing decaying bodies in the future and in the past.

I can't know this. I am only looking for a theory to fit the facts. That's what scientists do, though you may feel I am too far-fetched.

Perhaps I am.

Poisoned or not, the mercury has made me think like this. Drop it and it shivers in clones of itself all over the floor, but you can scoop it up again and there won't be any seams or shatter marks. It's one life or countless lives depending on what you want.

What do I want?

126

When I'm dreaming I want a home and a lover and some children, but it won't work. Who'd want to live with a monster? I may not look like a monster any more but I couldn't hide it for long. I'd break out, splitting my dress, throwing the dishes at the milkman if he leered at me and said, 'Hello, darling.' The truth is I've lost patience with this hypocritical stinking world. I can't take it any more. I can't flatter, lie, cajole, or even smile very much. What is there to smile about?

'You don't try,' my mother said. 'It's not so bad.'

It is so bad.

'You're pretty,' said my father, 'any man would want to marry you.'

Not if he pulled back my eyelids, not if he peeped into my ears, not if he looked down my throat with a torch, not if he listened to my heartbeat with a stethoscope. He'd run out of the room holding his head. He'd see her, the other one, lurking inside. She fits, even though she's so big.

I had sex with a man once: in out in out. A soundtrack of grunts and a big sigh at the end.

He said, 'Did you come?'

Of course I didn't come, haven't you read Master's and Johnson.

And then he fell asleep and his breathing was in out in out.

Later I said, 'I'd like to swallow you.'

'Adventurous, eh?' he said.

Whole, I meant, every single bit, straight down the throat like an oyster, your feet last, your feet waving in my mouth like a diver's flippers. Jonah and the Whale.

I don't hate men, I just wish they'd try harder. They all want to be heroes and all we want is for them to stay at home and help with the housework and the kids. That's not the kind of heroism they enjoy.

'You're so negative,' said my mother.

No I'm not, you are. You're the one who sits and watches the news and eats your factory-farmed meat and your battery eggs and chucks your endless stream of plastic into gouged out craters in the countryside. Where do you think all that rubbish goes?

I don't know if other worlds exist in space or time. Perhaps this is the only one and the rest is rich imaginings. Either way it doesn't matter. We have to protect both possibilities. They seem to be interdependent.

I have a memory of a time when I was a schoolgirl and getting fatter by the day. At that time we lived in a council flat on Upper Thames Street in London, by the river. Later we had our own home, but we were poor and working-class then. My mother forgets this was ever so. I was walking home from school by myself. I walked along the Embankment and watched the boats going up and down. There was a Punch and Judy ship and Mr Punch was bashing the baby and Judy was trying to strangle him and there was Toby the dog in his white ruff.

I didn't want to go home. I wanted to stay out all night and make a bed by the river and light a fire. I climbed up the steps at Waterloo Bridge and ignored the racing traffic so that I could look out on either side at St Paul's and Westminster. It wasn't easy: everyone wanted to get home, the view didn't matter. It was autumn and so the sun was setting early and the air was sharp. I liked it hurting my nostrils and making patterns when I blew out. I watched the sun sliding behind the buildings, and as I concentrated the screeching cars and the thudding people and the smells of rubber and exhaust receded. I felt I was alone on a different afternoon.

I looked at my forearms resting on the wall. They were massive, like thighs, but there was no wall, just a wooden spit, and when I turned in the opposite direction I couldn't see the dome of St Paul's.

I could see rickety vegetable boats and women arguing with one another and a regiment on horseback crossing the Thames.

I had to get on to Blackfriars, there was someone waiting for me.

Who? Who?

Now I wake up in the night shouting 'Who? Who?' like an owl.

Why does that day return and return as I sit by a rotting river with only the fire for company?

Morning. Out at sea the ship held at anchor. Jordan's rowing boat pulled high on the beach. The fire is smoking, it must be blazing when he wakes. In Hell the fires will blaze eternally, there'll be no scouring the sands for driftwood.

When Jordan stirs I've already collected a great pile of salvage and I am opening oysters with my little knife – a fine knife with an ebony handle got from a dead Sir Somebody who happened to be a Puritan. That was before I reformed myself. After the untimely end of Preacher Scroggs and Neighbour Firebrace I vowed to live quietly again and restrain my natural capacity for murder. I do not think of myself as a criminal, and indeed would protest any attempt to confine me in Newgate. My actions are not motivated by thought of gain, only by thought of justice, and I have searched my soul to conclude that there is no person dead at my hand who would be better off alive. As evidence, if any need evidence, I will cite the good wife of Preacher Scroggs, she whose only pleasure had been his member poking through a sheet. When she heard of the death of her husband (I was too ladylike to describe the circumstances themselves) she raised her hands to Heaven and thanked God for his mercy. Such is my humility that I bore no resentment at this mistaken gratitude towards Our Saviour. I wanted no thanks myself, and Our Lord is often robbed of His due. She packed up her things straight away and went to live with her unmarried sister in the town of Tunbridge Wells. I watched her go with tears in my eyes to think what she had suffered and from what horrors she had been released.

And if on Judgement Day it proves I have made a mistake once or a second time, I know Our Lord will wrap me to him as he did the woman taken in adultery and ask, 'Who will cast the first stone?'

When Jordan and myself had each swallowed thirty-six oysters he told me he must leave for London immediately to present the King with his rarest find.

'I have it here,' he said, 'in this bag, but before long it will perish.'

'Not gold, then?' I said, disappointed.

He laughed and assured me there was gold enough on the ship.

'Show me your wonder,' I said.

He unwrapped his bag as tenderly as I had unwrapped him on that first day in the broth-coloured Thames.

'I think it is another fruit,' I said, when I looked on its hide like that of a reptile and its spiky green crown of the kind that would grace an imp in Hell.

'Another fruit?' He seemed puzzled. I told him of our trip to visit the first banana and what a shock it had been in both shape and colour.

'Since that day,' said I, 'there's no fruit or vegetable can unsettle me.'

'I remember that day,' he said.

Then he jumped up and began to collect his things together.

'We will engage horses in the town.'

'And what horse will carry me?'

After some argument it was agreed that we should go to the expense of a carriage. It is my custom to walk everywhere, but as the mother of a hero come home I deemed it undignified to limp into London two days after my son and carrying my own baggage.

'Is your necklace also a precious thing?' I said, feigning only a small interest. He looked at me sharply and stopped his bustling.

'It was given to me by a woman who does not exist. Her name is Fortunata.'

'I knew an Italian pirate of that name once,' I said.

Jordan was staring out to sea. 'It was a day like this she

described, when she told me the story of Artemis and why she was in her service.'

'Tell it to me,' I said. 'It is only just light.'

FORTUNATA'S STORY

The goddess Artemis begged of her father, King Zeus, a bow and arrows, a short tunic and an island of her own free from interference. She didn't want to get married, she didn't want to have children. She wanted to hunt. Hunting did her good.

By morning she had packed and set off for a new life in the woods. Soon her fame spread and other women joined her, but Artemis didn't care for company. She wanted to be alone. In her solitude she discovered something very odd. She had envied men their long-legged freedom to roam the world and return full of glory to wives who only waited. She knew about the heroes and the home-makers, the great division that made life possible. Without rejecting it she had simply hoped to take on the freedoms of the other side, but what if she travelled the world and the seven seas like a hero? Would she find something different or the old things in different disguises?

The alchemists have a saying, '*Tertium non data*': the third is not given. That is, the transformation from one element to another, from waste matter into best gold, is a process that cannot be documented. It is fully mysterious. No one really knows what effects the change. And so it is with the mind that moves from its prison to a vast plain without any movement at all. We can only guess at what happened.

One evening when Artemis had lost her quarry she lit a fire and tried to rest, but the night was shadowy and full of games. She saw herself by the fire as a child, a woman, a hunter, a queen. Grabbing the child she lost sight of the woman, and when she drew her bow the queen fled. What would it matter if she crossed the world and hunted down every living creature so long as her separate selves eluded her? In the end when no one was left she would have to confront herself.

Then Orion came.

He wandered into Artemis' camp one day, scattering her dogs and bellowing like a bad actor, his right eye patched and his left arm in a splint. She was a mile or so away fetching water. When she returned she saw this huge rag of a man eating her goat. Raw. When he'd finished, with a great belch and the fat still fresh around his mouth, he suggested they take a short stroll by the sea's edge. Artemis didn't want to but she was frightened. His reputation hung around him like bad breath. He was, after all, the result of three of the gods in a good mood pissing on an ox-hide. And he was a mighty hunter.

The ragged shore, rock-pitted and dark with weed, reminded him of his adventures, and he unravelled them in detail while the tide came in up to her waist. There was nowhere he hadn't been, nothing he hadn't seen. He was faster than a hare and stronger than a pair of bulls. He was as good as a god.

'You smell,' said Artemis, but he didn't hear.

Eventually he allowed her to wade in from the rising water and light a fire for them both. He didn't want her to talk, he knew about her already, he'd been looking for her. She was a curiosity; he was famous. What a marriage.

But Artemis did talk. She talked about the land she loved and its daily changes. This was where she wanted to stay until she was ready to go. The journey itself was not enough. She got up to say goodbye. She turned.

Orion raped Artemis and fell asleep.

She thought about that time for years. It took just a few moments, and her only sensation was the hair on his stomach matted with sand.

Her revenge was swift and simple. She killed him with a scorpion.

In a night 200,000 years can pass, time moving only in our minds. The steady marking of the seasons, the land well-loved and always changing, continues outside, while inside light years revolve us under different skies.

Artemis lying beside dead Orion sees her past changed by a single act. The future is intact, still unredeemed, but the past is irredeemable. She is not who she thought she was. Every action and decision has led her here. The moment has

132

been waiting the way the top step of the stairs waits for the sleepwalker. She has fallen and now she is awake.

On the beach the waves made pools of darkness around Artemis' feet. She kept the fire burning, warming herself and feeling Orion grow slowly cold.

The fiery circle surrounding her held all the clues she needed to recognize that life is for a moment contained in one shape then released into another. Monuments and cities would fade away like the people who built them. No resting place or palace could survive the light years that lay ahead. There was no history that would not be rewritten and the earliest days were already too far away to see.

What would history make of tonight?

Tonight is clear and cold, the wind whipping the waves into peaks. The foam leaves slug trails in rough triangles on the sand. The salt smell bristles the hair inside her nostrils. Her lips are dry. The stars show her how to hang in space supported by nothing at all. Without medals or certificates or territories she owns, she can burn as they do, travelling through time until time has no meaning any more.

It's almost light. She wants to lie awake watching the night fade and the stars fade until the first grey-blue slates the sky. She wants to see the sun slash the water, but she can't stay awake for everything; some things have to pass her by. So what she doesn't see are the lizards coming out for food, or Orion's eyes turned glassy overnight. A small bird perches on his shoulder, trying to steal a piece of his famous hair.

Artemis waited until the sun was up before she trampled out the fire. She brought rocks and stones to cover Orion's body from the eagles. She made a high mound that broke the thudding wind as it scored the shore. It was a stormy day, black clouds and a thick orange shining on the horizon. By the time she had finished she was soaked with rain. Her hands were bleeding, her hair kept catching in her mouth. She was hungry but not angry now.

The sand that had been blond yesterday was now brown with wet. As far as she could see there was the grey water

133

white-edged and the birds of prey wheeling above it. Lonely cries, and she was lonely, not for friends but for a time that hadn't been violated. The sea was hypnotic. Not the wind or the cold could move her from where she sat like one who waited. She was not waiting, she was remembering. She was trying to find out what it was that had brought her here. What it was about herself. The third is not given. All she knew was that she had arrived at the frontiers of common sense and crossed over. She was safe now. No safety without risk, and what you risk reveals what you value.

She stood up and walked away, not looking behind her but conscious of her feet shaping themselves in the sand. Finally, at the headland, after a bitter climb to where the woods bordered the steep edge, she turned and stared out, seeing the shape of Orion's mound, just visible now, and her own footsteps walking away. Then it was fully night and she could see nothing to remind her of the night before, except the stars.

On our way back to London Jordan apologized to me for talking so little.

'It was never my way,' he said, 'nor yours either.'

I was perplexed by this, since I like to think of myself as a cheerful person, ever ready with some vital conversation. Had not Jordan and myself talked forever when he was a boy?

Then he said, 'On my travels I visited an Indian tribe known as the Hopi. I could not understand them, but in their company they had an old European man, Spanish, I think, though he spoke English to us. He said he had been captured by the tribe and now lived as one of them. I offered him passage home but he laughed in my face. I asked if their language had some similarity to Spanish and he laughed again and said, fantastically, that their language has no grammar in the way we recognize it. Most bizarre of all, they have no tenses for past, present and future. They do not sense time in that way. For them, time is one. The old man said it was impossible to learn their language without learning their world. I asked him how long it had taken him and he said that question had no meaning.'

After this we continued in silence.

Whilst Jordan was at the Crown of Thorns, dressing himself to present his pineapple to the King, I busied myself as a good woman should, cleaning the hut and brushing down the dogs. He had not seen his home for so long, and I wanted him to be surprised, for I have risen in the world myself these last years. I have begun to sell my dogs to the nobility, and I hope tonight to interest the King in a fine hound with ears that can hear across two counties and legs to make a concubine envious. I have fenced off a plot of garden at the front of my hut, and with all the skills I learned from Tradescant in those six years at Wimbledon I have made a fine greenery with a vine curling up the side wall.

I intend to hide the hound beneath my skirts, and when I am presented to the King I will let it out a little and throw myself on his mercy, acting as though I had not known it to be there. Then, if all goes as it should by rights, the King will weigh the dog's head and note the eager slant of his body and his tail like a weather-vane in the wind. Then he will ask me if he can buy it and I shall become coy as I am able and refuse and refuse, saying he is only a pet. The price will rise, I know, and then all the rest of the silly sheep will follow suit of the King and order more hounds than I can breed. I see I have a flair for enterprise. It was ever with me, but smothered, I think, under my maternalness and the pressing need to do away with scoundrels.

There is something to be said for this childless quiet life.

And now the bells are striking and I must drape on my pearls and get ready for Jordan. I have washed my neck.

Jack said, 'The trouble with you, Nicolas, is that you never think about your future, you just live day to day.'

He was visiting me on board *HMS Gauntlet*. He was smart and confident. He was the youngest stock analyst in the City. I looked at him mildly and he continued.

'You'll be out of the Navy in a year or so and you don't know what you want to do. You'll turn into a loser, Nicolas, I'm only trying to help you.'

'Do you remember those afternoons in the park, Jack? You always brought your computer magazines and your father's copies of *GP*. One week you brought a canvas windshield and lay with your face to the sun.'

'And you brought those boat things.'

'This is a boat thing, Jack, only bigger.'

'You can't make a career out of a hobby, Nicolas.'

And you? And you?

I tried to make sense of him as he sat at my table, his face in a scowl, his hands fiddling with the newspaper he'd got out of his briefcase. Outside sleet smeared the window.

'If you really want to know, I'm thinking of sailing round the world. The same route as Drake took in the *Golden Hind*. I'm going to do it alone.'

Jack looked up and gave me a flicker of attention.

'Will you break some record or other?'

'How should I know?'

He stood up and threw down the paper.

'See what I mean? Even when you have a chance to do something useful you don't. What's the point of sailing round the bloody world if you're not going to break a record? You could go round the world in a plane if that's all you want.'

'I want to sail it. They used to think, certainly Christopher Columbus used to think, that the world was five-sixths land

and one-sixth water. It says so in Esdras, a book of the Apocrypha. It's two-thirds water, though. You wouldn't know that if you travelled everywhere by plane. Planes make you think the world's solid.'

'And I think the world's divided into two sorts of people. Those who do and those who won't do.'

'And I won't do, Jack?'

He didn't answer, just fixed on the paper. Then he swore.

'Stupid, some woman's at it again.'

He started storming round the cabin, smacking at the sleet sticking to the outside of the window, with his rolled-up-newspaper.

'You'll never hit them,' I said, 'they're on the other side.'

It was the wrong thing to say. He launched into a tirade against all of us who were holding up progress and industry and the free market.

'Stupid woman's camping by some tiny river in the middle of nowhere and moaning on about the mercury levels. What does she want? Does she think industry can just pack up and go home? They've got to put it somewhere. It's not as though they're chucking it in the Thames.'

At this risk of sounding like the Buddha, I said, 'All rivers run into the sea.'

He didn't hear me. He opened the paper again.

'There's going to be television programme about her, and an inquiry. God, the media's irresponsible. People are stupid. They panic. Before you know it they'll be selling shares and the company'll probably go under. And why? For some loony housewife and a few fish.'

'I don't know what's the matter with you, Jack.'

He came close and swung the chair round so that he was sitting on it cowboy style.

'I'll tell you what's the matter. I work twelve, fifteen hours a day at what I'm good at and I'm getting tired of nosy people poking about in the private business of perfectly respectable companies. Everybody wants jobs and money. How do they think we make jobs and money? There's always some fall-out, some consequence we'd rather not have, but you do have them and that's life.'

He checked his watch. 'I have to go now. Come to lunch some time?'

I nodded. He threw his paper at me. 'Here, keep up with the world, even if you don't want to join it.'

I flattened the springy newspaper when he'd gone and tried to find the article which had upset him. I remembered something he'd said after I'd decided to join up – what was it?

'Typical of you to make a career in the Navy after the Falklands crisis.'

I read the article. Surely this woman was a hero? Heroes give up what's comfortable in order to protect what they believe in or to live dangerously for the common good. She was doing that, so why was she being persecuted? The article said her tent had been mysteriously fired at on a number of occasions. I tried to understand her through her photograph. She was pretty; I felt I knew her, though this was not possible. Before I realized it I stood up and took down my kit bag.

I would find her.

God's judgement on the murder of the King has befallen us. London is consumed by the Plague. The city is thick with the dead. There are bodies in every house and in a street south of here the only bodies are dead ones. The houses are deserted, their shutters banging open in the night.

I took some soup to an ailing friend of mine, and as I kicked on the door to open it I saw the cart making its way slowly down the street, filling with corpses as it went. The men who pushed it were convicts. If they survived their daily labour they would be granted their freedom at the end of one month. Newgate was emptying but no criminals roared in their new-found liberty.

The men were bent double, the street was rutted and pot-holed and as the cart became heavier they could hardly move it. They were thin and ragged themselves, and one had the greenish hue that is the sure sign of rot.

I put down my soup and made to help them. I have no fear of the Plague. My body is too big for sour-sickness to defeat it, and if it is a judgement on us all then surely I am the last to be judged?

I went in every house and pulled out bodies stiff with death. Most were wrapped in filthy blankets but some were still on their knees in the attitude of prayer. A grisly sight they looked, propped up in the cart, hands together.

At my friend's house I went inside with the soup, expecting to find her as I had left her, weak but tolerable. She was dead.

The carters were so exhausted by this time that we sat together round her table and ate the soup.

'Where are you taking the bodies?' I asked.

'To be burned,' they said. 'There is no way but burning. The grave-diggers have no strength left, there are too many for them. Only the moneyed may be buried. For us it is the pit.'

I went with them to the pit, carrying my friend over my shoulder. I wanted her going to be more dignified than it could have been in the cart. The closer we got, the more terrible became the smell. Dark smoke curled from a crater of the kind that must be on the moon. Around the edges of the pit were numerous carts which were tipped in from time to time. As soon as they were empty the miserable carters trundled away with them back to the foul streets.

Holding my nose with one hand, and keeping my friend secure with the other, I went and looked in. It was very deep and criss-crossed with huge pieces of wood, full trees here and there. In between, and sometimes caught in the branches, were the legs and arms and heads of the dead.

'It is a vision of Hell,' I said.

There was a man next to me who had some charge over the matter.

'It is Hell indeed, and this is work for imps. I must keep the fire burning to purify the rot of the bodies. Should it smoulder, myself and my men must take that cut stairway you see to the side and invigorate the flames with bellows. We have levelled a ridge round the inside of the crater to stand on. In this way we are able to walk fully round it and if necessary prod in any who are too close to the air.'

'I have brought my friend,' I said.

'Then you must cast her in and not look back.'

'I will carry her down. It is an indignity to be tossed aside.'

He tried to dissuade me, on account of the prodigious heat, but I made my way down step by step, my eyes running at the smoke and the fumes. When I reached the ledge I walked round until I saw a calm and pleasant branch not yet suffused in fire. Leaning, I laid her on it and made my ascent. The grim workers looked at me silently and turned back to their dreadful task.

When I got home Jordan was lying on his bed delirious with fever. He could hardly speak to me, and when he did his talk was of wild places and strange customs, and over and over again he repeated, 'Fortunata, Fortunata.'

I am a resourceful woman and believe I can do almost anything if it falls within the mortal realm, but I could not find a woman who did not exist.

In despair I went to the dog kennel and shook it with both hands until my neighbour poked her head out, cursing such oaths as should never be heard in female company.

'You must pay me my due for kindness,' I said. 'My boy is dying. He must live.'

She started her cackling and muttering and nonsense about those who must accept the will of God, and was making to go back in when I snatched her by the waist and held her up over my head.

Make him well,' I said, as politely as I could, 'otherwise I may not say what maternal rage might do.'

I put her down and went inside to bathe Jordan's head and feed him oranges. He could have been a lord had he wished it. The King wanted to heap honours on him and would have equipped him with any ship to sail the seas. But Jordan would not. He said he wanted to sit by the river and watch the boats. There were looks then; they could not understand him, and some whispered that he had gone mad in his thirteen years away. Others said his heart was broken. I listened and took not too much notice, for will not people always say something in preference to keeping quiet?

At night-time she came in with an evil-smelling pan of fluid and set it on the hearth.

'Let him drink it, bathe in it and sleep within sight of it,' was all she said, and then she scuttled back to her bed of bones. I heard her crunching in the dark.

We did as she demanded, and after a few days Jordan's fever abated and he was well enough to eat a chop.

'We should thank her,' he said, and took her a ruby. She held it to the light and squinted at it, then, satisfied it was genuine, she exclaimed on its good properties for the blood and ate it. Jordan and myself were very much taken aback but we went inside without a word.

When the Plague was over, in 1665, London was a quieter place and there were plenty of houses to be had. I approved of being able to go to market without having to fight through a Godless stream of foolish persons. But a strange sickness had come over me, not of the body, but of the mind. I fancied that I still smelt the stench wherever I went. I couldn't rid my nostrils of the odour of death. I began to think of London as a place full of filth and pestilence that would never be clean.

'God's revenge is still upon us,' I said to Jordan. 'We are corrupt and our city is corrupted. There is no whole or beautiful thing left . . .'

Then Jordan announced, suddenly and without warning, that he was intending to put to sea again and had prepared a vessel at Deptford.

'Will you go at once?' I asked, full of fear.

'Not at once, but when I must go I shall be ready.'

Hearing this I set out around the streets, walking for comfort, but wherever I walked carried the same message. That this rot would not be purged. And I thought of the fire in the pit and of all the bodies whose ashes at least were clean.

'This city should be burned down,' I whispered to myself.

'It should burn and burn until there is nothing left but the cooling wind.'

'My name is Nicolas Jordan,' I said.

We ate supper from her campfire: baked potatoes and beans and tin mugs of tea. She didn't want to talk much so we sat back to back watching the stars.

'The river's glowing,' I said.

'It's phosphorus, the tests are conclusive.'

'It reminds me of *The Ancient Mariner*, the slimy sea.'

She had a rowing boat tied to a tree, and we took it out and floated on the eery water, the orange of the campfire burning in the distance. I wanted to thank her for trying to save us, for trying to save me, because it felt that personal, though I don't know why. But when I tried to speak my throat was clogged with feelings that resist words. There's a painting I love called *The Sower*, by Van Gogh. A peasant walks home at evening with a huge yellow moon behind him. The land is strong and certain, made of thick colours laid on with a palette knife. It comforts me because it makes me think that the world will always be here, strong and certain, at the end of a day, at the end of a journey. Brown fields and a yellow moon.

'Let's burn it,' she said. 'Let's burn down the factory.'

On September the second, in the year of Our Lord, sixteen hundred and sixty-six, a fire broke out in a baker's yard in Pudding Lane. The flames were as high as a man, and quickly spread to the next house and the next. I had been drinking with my friends the bakers all night, or, rather, they had been drinking and it was fortunate for them that I was able to pull their bodies to a safe place. I did not start the fire – how could I, having resolved to lead a blameless life? – but I did not stop it. Indeed the act of pouring a vat of oil on to the flames may well have been said to encourage it. But it was a sign, a sign that our great sin would finally be burned away. I could not have hindered the work of God.

I ran home and awaited news. The fire was moving westwards. A day later it seemed the whole of London was burning.

'Hurry, Jordan,' I said, 'we have done with this time and place.'

We packed our things and left for his ship. I would gladly have taken the dog kennel and its occupant, but she would not come. We made her a raft from a chicken crate and left her staring at the smoke-filled sky.

The river was filling with people and their belongings. On Jordan's instructions I rowed down the Thames while he attended to some final arrangements. I waited for him until nightfall, and still he did not come and did not come, and then the descending fog robbed me of all view except the flames.

About half an hour after midnight I heard him come aboard. His face was pale, his hands trembled. I thought it was the devastation he had seen, but he shook his head. He was coming through London Fields when the fog covered him and, hurrying, he had fallen and banged his head. He came to, and feeling his way, arms outstretched he had suddenly touched another face and screamed out. For a second the fog cleared and he saw that the stranger was himself.

'Perhaps I am to die,' he said, and then, while I was protesting this, 'Or perhaps I am to live, to be complete as she said I would be.'

'Who is this she?'

'Fortunata.'

I did not answer him, and he sprang away and cast off from the bank. The ship eased out into the darkness and in a few hours we had left behind the livid flames and the terrible sound of burning. We slid peacefully towards the sea, the wind behind us, the great sail fat. I looked at Jordan standing in the prow, his silhouette black and sharp-edged. I thought I saw someone standing beside him, a woman, slight and strong. I tried to call out but I had no voice. Then she vanished and there was nothing next to Jordan but empty space.

As I drew my ship out of London I knew I would never go there again. For a time I felt only sadness, and then, for no reason, I was filled with hope. The future lies ahead like a glittering city, but like the cities of the desert disappears when approached. In certain lights it is easy to see the towers and the domes, even the people going to and fro. We speak of it with longing and with love. *The future*. But the city is a fake. The future and the present and the past exist only in our minds, and from a distance the borders of each shrink and fade like the borders of hostile countries seen from a floating city in the sky. The river runs from one country to another without stopping. And even the most solid of things and the most real, the best-loved and the well-known, are only hand-shadows on the wall. Empty space and points of light.